THE CASE OF THE SAD MISCHIEVOUS GHOST

I0658795

(DAVEY & DEREK JUNIOR DETECTIVES SERIES, BOOK 5)

JANICE SPINA

Copyright 2017

By Janice Spina
All rights reserved

DEDICATION

To my two middle grandsons, Jason and Joey, who love to read about mysteries and adventures and inspire me to write more

ACKNOWLEDGEMENTS

Thank you to my beta readers, John Spina, Michele Rolfe, and Michelle Clement James for their tireless efforts to read and review this book and for their helpful input.

A special thank you to my husband, John, for the lovely chapter illustrations and the beautiful cover of this book.

OTHER BOOKS BY JANICE SPINA:

Pre-School to Grade Three:

Louey the Lazy Elephant

Ricky the Rambunctious Raccoon

Jerry the Crabby Crayfish (Won Pinnacle Book Achievement Award)

Lamby the Lonely Lamb

(Received Silver Medal from Mom's Choice Awards)

Jesse the Precocious Polar Bear

Broose the Moose on the Loose

Sebastian Meets Marvin the Monkey

Colby the Courageous Cat

Jeffrey the Jittery Giraffe

Middle-Grade/Preteen:

The Case of the Missing Cell Phone

(Davey & Derek Junior Detectives Series, Book 1)

(Won Pinnacle Book Achievement Award & Reader's Favorite Book)

The Case of the Mysterious Black Cat

(Davey & Derek Junior Detectives Series, Book 2)

(Won Pinnacle Book Achievement Award)

The Case of the Magical Ivory Elephant

(Davey & Derek Junior Detectives Series, Book 3)

(Won Pinnacle Book Achievement Award)

The Case of the Brown Scraggly Dog

(Davey & Derek Junior Detectives Series, Book 4)

<u>Novels: (under J.E. Spina)</u>

Hunting Mariah

How Far Is Heaven

An Angel Among Us (A Short Story Collection)

Table of Contents

INTRODUCTION

Davey and Derek Donato, now eleven years old, are twins but not identical. They each have their own distinct talents and are junior detectives by their own design. They live in the quiet town of Lindon, New Hampshire where nothing much happens, reason why the boys look for adventures.

They gleaned the idea to be detectives from a book their parents bought each of them for their tenth birthday on July 15th.

Davey, with black hair and green eyes, is the older twin by three minutes and teases his brother all the time about being the baby brother. He is patient and caring and an intellectual who likes to sleep late. He has the ability where anything he reads can be committed to memory. This is extremely helpful when he has to help Derek who hasn't done the required reading for school ahead of time. Davey also likes to take things apart in order to find out how they work.

Derek, with light brown hair and green eyes, on the other hand, is a thinker and somewhat of a dreamer but an early riser. He thinks things through and likes to be in control and see things running smoothly. He excels in writing, math and problem solving. He does have an aptitude for getting into all kinds of trouble by himself. Trouble, unfortunately, seems to follow him, but luckily Davey always backs Derek up.

The boys also have a friend, Mickey Catonni, aka Cat, with wiry red hair, who helped the boys in their first case,

The Case of the Missing Cell Phone.
Mickey is a cool kind of kid who has a fun personality, great sense of humor and gets along well with others.

The twins began their cases as junior detectives in ***Book 1, The Case of the Missing Cell Phone*** when they helped an older student discover what happened to her mother's cell phone.

Mickey has a little sister, Jenny, who is deaf. Knowing sign language helps Mickey to talk with Jenny. Jenny plays an important part in ***Book 2, The Case of the Mysterious Black Cat***. In this book the boys discover magic and learn the secret that their Great Aunt Gigi has kept.

There are more magical adventures in ***Book 3, The Case of the Magical Ivory***

Elephant where the unexpected happens to Davey and Derek.

The adventures continue in ***Book 4, The Case of the Brown Scraggly Dog*** when the boys discover a mystery involving a dog with blood on its paw.

THE CASE OF THE SAD MISCHIEVOUS GHOST

(DAVEY & DEREK JUNIOR DETECTIVES SERIES, BOOK 5)

Written by Janice Spina

Illustrations and Cover by John Spina

Published by Janice Spina 2017

CHAPTER ONE

New Year at School

Davey tossed and turned and finally got up when he heard his brother's voice once again.

"Hey Davey, time to get up! First day back to school!" Derek yelled for the second time as he bounded into his brother's room.

Davey hated for the summer to end. He and Derek had had a great summer with their new dog, Aggy.

"Derek, can you please keep the noise down a few decibels? I can't take your loud voice first thing in the morning. I'm up, okay?" Davey sighed and rummaged around for his clothes as he locked gazes with his brother and gave him the eerie eyeball.

"Oh boy, Davey. I know that look. You don't have to give me the eerie eyeball! I got the picture and the message, the whole shebang! It's not too pretty!" Derek laughed his way out of his brother's room.

Derek's laughter could be heard as he went down the stairs which grated on

Davey's nerves as he quickly got dressed. Davey heaved another big sigh and finally joined Derek at the kitchen table.

"Well, here he is! Sleeping ugly has arrived!" Derek couldn't help but get on his brother's nerves once again.

"Okay boys, enough is enough! Eat your breakfast. It's getting late. I have to get to work earlier today. Make sure you go over to Aunt Gigi's after school. You can come home to get your bikes, let Aggy out and lock up again. I will call you when I get home. I may be a little later today because I have to stop at the supermarket to pick up something for dinner. Behave yourself in school and for your aunt. Do you hear me?"

Both boys nodded and mumbled, "Okay Mom," and went back to shoveling in their breakfast.

Once the twins arrived at school Davey had finally woken up. He was not a morning person and hated getting up early. He managed to sleep later during the summer in spite of Derek's efforts to wake him up earlier.

Derek poked Davey as they headed to their home room to begin the day. "Are you awake yet, Bro?"

"Hey, cut it out, Derek. Of course I'm awake," Davey chirped up and poked his brother back in jest.

The boys looked over their schedules and grumbled when they both noticed simultaneously that they had Mr. Colton for Math.

"Oh no, Davey! Look who we have for math! I heard that he is a crazy man when it comes to homework. You better pay close attention for both of us in case I zone out," Derek chuckled.

"I don't think you will have any trouble with math, Derek. You may have to give me some help.

"Now that is funny, Davey! You never want help with anything...but wait a minute, you always require help getting up in the morning!" Derek punched his brother's arm and ran ahead to their next class.

The day moved slowly and the twins went from classroom to classroom picking up their books, supplies and homework, especially in math. The boys hurried to lunch and grabbed as much as they could put onto their trays.

Derek always took extra dessert while Davey wanted extra bread. The lunch attendants always made sure the boys got all they wanted. The twins were favorites of all the lunch ladies because the boys were always so good-mannered.

Davey looked around the room and noticed two girls staring at him and his brother. He poked Derek and said, "Hey don't look now but two girls over there are coming this way."

"Huh, what girls, Davey? Are they cute?"

"Shh, they are almost here."

Derek looked up from his lunch and quickly swallowed his food before turning to look at the girls who were standing next to Davey.

"Um, hello. Are you Davey and Derek Donato, the junior detectives?" the girl with the curly brown hair and green eyes asked.

"Hi, yep, that's us," Davey announced as he looked the girls over for a clue why they were asking this.

"Hi, I'm Abby and this is my cousin, Holly."

"Hi Abby and Holly. I'm Davey and this is my brother, Derek," he said as he smiled to put the girls at ease. But soon felt a little uncomfortable when he looked at Abby's big green eyes.

Derek glanced at the girls and mumbled, "Hi," and went back to eating.

"Sorry to disrupt your lunch but we have to talk to you about a problem we have or I have, that is. I haven't shared this with anyone else yet."

Davey had been giving the girls all his attention. When Derek heard that they had a problem, he perked up too.

Derek pushed forward and asked, "What problem?"

Abby looked at Holly and nodded and continued. "We recently moved here from North Carolina and my dad bought this house in Linden a few blocks from school. It's the Sheridan House."

Davey looked at Derek and whistled out loud but quickly quieted down when one of the teachers looked his way.

"Oh, wow, no one has lived there for a long time. Could be fifty years or more," Derek announced.

What's going on there? Have you had visitors?" Davey asked as he tapped the table nervously with his fork.

"Well, let's say that we have had some visitations and unexplained happenings lately," Abby explained.

Davey couldn't contain his excitement over this news about the visitations. He interrupted by saying, "Listen, Abby. We can come over to your house and check it out sometime. Is that what you want us to do?"

Derek was watching the girls' expression as he waited for Abby to answer.

"Well, if that would be okay with your parents. My mom is home all the time and my dad is working out of state at the moment. I'm sure Mom won't mind if I bring you over after school one day."

Holly stepped forward and said, "Yes, that would be great if you guys could come over to Abby's house. I am staying there until my parents return from a business trip overseas. I'm nervous about being there but I have nowhere else to go."

"Oh Holly, don't worry these guys will help us. As long as we stick together we will figure how to get rid of the unwanted guests."

"Yeah, I guess," Holly sighed.

"Listen, Abby, we need to check with our Aunt Gigi. We go there after school every day since our mother works. But I think she will let us go over to your house. We can ride our bikes there. Can you give me your phone number and

I'll call you and set up a day and time? Oh, and Abby, don't worry we won't share this with anyone else except our friend and fellow detective, Mickey Catonni."

"Okay as long as he doesn't tell anyone else. We don't want to attract a lot of attention. Here's my address and phone number." Abby wrote her information on a napkin and handed it to Davey. As Abby started to walk away she turned back and said, "Look forward to hearing from you, Davey. Thanks."

Derek watched Holly with her long straight blonde hair and blue eyes walk away. He was looking forward to going to their house.

Davey was looking at Abby and thinking the same thing as his brother as he announced, "Hey Derek, they are pretty cute, huh?"

"They're okay. But I am more interested in going to their house to see whatever they are seeing."

"Are you afraid to say the word, ghost, Derek?"

"No, not really, but I don't know if they are real or only in our imagination."

"What do you think, Davey?"

"I think they are real if we think they are real. Besides, let's see for ourselves when we get there, okay, Bro?"

"Yeah, okay. We better finish up or we may get into trouble, Davey. Oh no, Mr. Colton is heading this way."

The boys grabbed their snacks first, emptied their trays and headed out of the café before Mr. Colton could catch up to them.

CHAPTER TWO

New Case

The twins discussed their new case in hushed tones on the bus, including Cat in their plans.

"Hey, can I come over to the girls' house too? You're going to need me for my charming personality. I will win the ghost over especially if it's a girl."

Davey shushed Cat when he said ghost out loud. "Cat, this is a secret. No one knows about this. The girls haven't shared this with anyone else. Meet at our house as soon as you can, Cat."

"Okay, no problem, Davey. My lips are sealed." Cat motioned zipping up his lips.

At their stops the boys rushed out of the bus and headed home to get their bikes. Aggy was happy to see them and raced around the yard not in a hurry to do her business.

"Come one Aggy, hurry up. We have things to do. We will play with you later." Derek put Aggy back in the house, tossed her a couple of dog biscuits, and locked up feeling a little guilty for rushing her.

The twins used "TT" (twin telepathy) to continue discussing what they would do about talking to Aunt Gigi when they got to her house.

Maybe we should let Cat talk to her. He has such charm, or so he thinks.

Yeah, funny, Derek! We can't invite Cat. We didn't ask Mom if we could have him come with us to Aunt Gigi's. We should go in alone and talk to Aunt Gigi quickly and ask if we can go to Cat's house.

We ought to tell Aunt Gigi the truth, Davey. You know what happens when we don't. Aunt Gigi will know. She knows when we are lying or trying to hide things. I don't want to see her eyes get like they did once before. I thought she was going to turn you into a pig or something worse or even burn you up.

Yes, Derek, I do remember that. I will never forget it!

Oops, here comes Cat.

"Hi guys! What's up? You look like you were discussing something heavy without me. Did I miss out on something important?"

"Nah, nothing new, Cat. We were discussing how we're going to ask Aunt Gigi if we can go over to Abby's house. Of course, we should find out if she will let us go today if that is okay with Abby," Derek spoke up first.

"Well, let's go. Time's a wasting!" Cat raced ahead.

Davey and Derek raced alongside Cat, giving him a little competition.

Tires screeched as the three boys arrived outside Aunt Gigi's house. Aunt Gigi was at the front window watching the boys as she sipped her tea. She knew something was up by the way they raced up her stairs.

Aunt Gigi opened the door and welcomed the boys in with open arms. But as always they were ready for her and deftly ducked under her arms and ran to the kitchen escaping once again from one of her bone-crushing hugs.

Uncle George was sitting at the table having a cup of coffee as he looked up and smiled. "Hey boys, how are you doing?"

"We're good, Uncle George. How are you doing?" Davey asked courteously.

"Pretty good for an old man," Uncle George laughed as his eyes twinkled.

Aunt Gigi entered behind the boys and went about preparing a snack for them.

"Aren't you going to invite your friend, Mickey, in for a snack too, boys?"

"Oh, is that okay, Aunt Gigi?" Derek asked with a surprised expression on his face.

"Of course, dear boys. Mickey is always welcome here. Go get him." Aunt Gigi motioned with her arms to the boys to hurry up.

Cat was even more surprised when he came into the kitchen after the boys' invitation and sat down to a splendid array of snacks. His eyes couldn't get any bigger.

"Thank you, Aunt Gigi, for inviting me. This is so cool! You make the best snacks! Oh, sorry, I called you Aunt

Gigi!" Cat's face showed his shock at his audacity.

"Oh, no problem, Mickey. I can be your adoptive aunt. That is quite all right dear boy," Aunt Gigi replied with a smile.

The twins watched their aunt for any signs that she was upset. They both sighed in relief and shared "TT".

That was kind of pushy of Cat, huh, Davey?

Yeah, I was surprised he would say that. But of course, he doesn't really know Aunt Gigi like we do.

Aunt Gigi called out to the twins, "Come sit down and stop talking in your heads. How's my favorite dog? Why didn't you bring Aggy too?"

Cat looked up quickly from his snacks with a puzzled expression. "Do you guys really talk to each other in your heads?"

"Yeah, I guess we do, Cat. We never told you that before. It's a twin thing. Can't help it. It happens all the time. Whatever I am thinking Derek soon thinks it too and vice versa."

"Wow that is way cool. I wish I had a twin. I could talk all the time with him and my mother would never know what we said."

"Yeah but our mother caught on to it already. She knows we do it all the time. It drives her crazy." Derek winked at Cat and laughed.

"Oh, sorry, Aunt Gigi, I didn't answer your question about Aggy. She's great. Mom didn't say we could bring her over here. Maybe next time. Aggy loves you too!"

"I hope you do. I miss my Aggy girl!"

Davey sat quietly as Derek chatted with Aunt Gigi and Cat. He was preparing to ask Aunt Gigi about the girls' house.

"Aunt Gigi, we met two girls in school today that live in the Sheridan house. Do you know anything about the house?" Davey leaned forward anticipating something that would help pave the way for them to go there.

"Hmm, the Sheridan house, you say. Yes, I remember the Sheridan's. Well, I mean, I know who they were. They lived here over fifty-five years ago. Mrs. Sheridan died tragically when she fell down the cellar stairs. Mr. Sheridan lived for several years after her but moved to a nursing home. He was too weak and ill to stay alone in that big house."

"Why do you ask, Davey?"

"Well, two girls, Abby and Holly, who are cousins live there. They moved in recently. They're in the sixth grade with us. We met them at lunch and…"

Derek picked up from there, "Yeah, they invited us over to their house. They said there have been strange things happening and unexpected visitors, like ghosts."

Davey continued, "Can we go over to their house sometime, maybe today if Abby's mother says okay? The girls asked for our help to get rid of the ghosts."

"I see. They require your help as detectives. So, this is your new case boys? Good for you. I don't see why not. But make sure you are back here before it gets dark. I will call your mother when she gets home if you are not."

"Oh, definitely we will get back here way before that, Aunt Gigi. Thank you so much!" Davey and Derek replied in tandem.

"Did you hear that Cat? Aunt Gigi said we can go over to Abby's house today. I better call her right now to see if her mother approves too."

Davey picked up the wall phone and dialed Abby's number and waited.

"Hello."

"Hi, can I speak to Abby please?"

"Who is calling? This is her mother, Mrs. Rizzo."

"Oh, hello, Mrs. Rizzo. This is Davey Donato. I met Abby in school today. We're in the same grade."

"Hmm, I see. Hold on a minute, Davey."

Davey let out a sigh and hoped that Mrs. Rizzo would agree to let them all go over today. She sounded so serious and stern.

"Hi Davey. Glad you called. I was going to ask Mom about having you guys come over. Hold on a minute please."

Davey waited as he heard mumbling on the other end of the phone but couldn't make out what was being said.

"Okay, it's all set, Davey. You can come over any time."

"That's great. I was calling to say that my Aunt Gigi said okay for us too. We'll be there shortly. We are bringing our friend, Cat, too. Okay?"

"Sure, I'll tell my mom. What's one more? Oh, Davey, don't say anything about the things I told you at school. I told Mom that you were coming over to help us with our math. Okay?"

"Um, sure, Okay. But we don't have our books with us."

"That's all right. You can use ours to explain things. We really do need help by the way. I wasn't kidding about that. Mr. Colton is really tough. He gave us a ton of homework. Did you do yours yet?"

"No, but we will do it with you while we talk over the other things. Okay?"

"Sure. See you soon, Davey."

CHAPTER THREE

Sheridan House

Abby and Holly were excited to welcome the boys and waited at the front door for them. Abby hinted to Holly, "I kind of like Davey. He's cute and so courteous."

"Well, I like Derek. He is a little shy and nervous when he's speaking. It could be because he isn't used to talking to girls."

"I guess that could be it," Abby remarked.

"Oh, they're here, Holly. Open the door quickly," Abby announced clearly excited.

She smoothed her hair back and smiled before saying, "Hi boys. Come on in. Nice to see you again." Abby made sure to meet Davey's eyes as she said this.

Davey smiled back at her and "TT" was exchanged with Derek.

Oh, Derek, I think she likes me too!

Yeah, guess so, Bro. Lucky you! Ha!

The boys quickly recovered from this exchange and walked into the living room where they met Mrs. Rizzo.

Abby quickly introduced the boys to her mother and observed them shaking her mother's hand and smiling graciously.

"Well, hello, boys. Nice to meet you. Can you please go wash your hands and go out to the kitchen? I have some snacks waiting for you."

"Oh, thank you, Mrs. Rizzo," Davey responded and he raised his eyebrows at his brother.

I don't think I can eat another thing. How about you Derek?

Well, that depends upon what the snacks are.

Look at Cat! He is ready for round two!

The twins looked at Cat who was washing his hands quickly and hurrying out of the bathroom to find the kitchen.

The girls were already sitting having some peanut butter on crackers and cream cheese and celery.

Cat sat down and dug right in. There was always room for more when it came to snacks. Cat smiled and winked at the twins as he popped another cracker with peanut butter into his mouth.

The twins each took a celery stalk with cream cheese and chewed slowly as they smiled at the girls.

The boys looked at each other and shared "TT".

Don't look now, but Cat is stuffing his face. I can't believe him, Davey!

I don't know where he puts it all.

We better not talk like this. The girls are looking at us strangely.

Well, at least you don't have that goofy face on.

Speak for yourself, Davey!

Ha! Later, Bro.

Abby turned toward Davey and asked, "So what do you think about Mr. Colton's class? I don't know what he is talking about when he gets technical about math problems. Can you explain these to me, Davey?"

"Sure, Abby." Davey leaned over the textbook and reviewed each problem.

Holly pushed her chair next to Derek and asked him some of her own questions about their homework.

"Derek, can you help me too? I am confused about this problem. I hate word problems and pre-Algebra. I can't understand why we should learn this. We will never use it. Right?" Holly batted her eyes at Derek clearly making him uncomfortable.

"Um, I guess we may use it one day. But it really isn't too bad. Let me explain this first one and you will understand the rest easier." Derek picked up a pencil and began to work out the first problem. He was in his element with the math problems at which he excelled.

Cat was busy eating his share of the crackers and celery and drinking his second glass of milk when he suddenly burped out loud. "Oh, excuse me. I guess I had enough. Thank you, Mrs. Rizzo," Mickey said as he wiped his mouth and brought his dish over to the sink much to Mrs. Rizzo's surprise.

"Well, aren't you a nice boy to clean up after yourself. I wish some other people would do the same thing around here." Mrs. Rizzo looked over at her daughter as she said this. But Abby was too engrossed in her math homework with Davey to hear her.

"My mother expects me to do that all the time. If I don't…well, I don't want to find out if I don't." Mickey smiled at Mrs. Rizzo and sat down next to the others and listened to the math lessons.

Mickey leaned over to Davey and whispered in his ear. "When are we going to see the ghosts?"

"Ssh, Cat, when the girls are ready to tell us more. We should finish up the homework first. Do you want to do yours too? Here's a paper and pencil."

"Nah, I'll do it when I get home."

Mickey looked around and noticed the kitchen was off the hallway that led to the living room and bathroom. He got up from his seat and walked back by the bathroom and peeked around the corner past the living room. There was another room that was filled with shelves and books like a library.

Walking further down the corridor he came to three doors and a stairway going up. He wanted to open each door but knew that it wouldn't be right to do that in someone's house. He was about to turn around and head back to the kitchen when he felt a cold breeze go past him. He looked around but didn't notice a window opened.

Mickey pulled his sweater tighter around him and walked briskly back to the kitchen as he kept turning to look behind him. He definitely felt as if someone was watching him. He looked up at the wall at pictures of some old people. Their eyes appeared to be following him.

When Mickey entered the kitchen he announced to the group, "Hey, I think I'll be going. I have to get home to do my homework before my mother comes home. See you. Thanks for the snacks, Mrs. Rizzo."

"Oh, you are most welcome, Mickey. Hope to see you again." Mrs. Rizzo went back to folding her clothes in the next room.

Davey and Derek looked up at Mickey and said, "Hey, why are you in such a hurry all of a sudden? Are you okay?"

Derek watched Mickey as he shook his head and said, "No, I don't feel well. I guess I ate too many snacks. See you girls tomorrow. Talk to you guys later."

Mickey ran out the door, jumped on his bike, and raced away looking behind him once again.

Derek used "TT" with Davey.

What's wrong with Cat? He's acting strangely. Did you notice his face? It was white.

I know. We should call him once we get home. Something happened to him. I wonder if he saw a ghost.

Yeah, he was only here for a little while. He could have been looking around and the ghost caught up to him.

After the boys and girls finished their homework Davey asked, "Abby, can we look around a little? Mickey left. I think he may have come into contact with your ghost."

"Oh, Mickey did look a little white. I guess he could have seen it. Sorry about that. I've never seen it during the day. It always comes at night."

Abby went into the laundry room next door to talk to her mother, "Mom, can I show the boys around the house?"

"Sure, honey but no staying in your room. You know the rules. Show them around then they will have to leave."

"Okay, Mom. Thanks."

Davey and Derek waited and shared "TT" until Abby came back. Holly was not aware that the boys were talking inside their heads because she talked non-stop to them about the house.

"What did you say, Holly?" Derek stopped using "TT" as he looked at her.

"Huh, oh, I said I felt a cold spot in the hall this morning. It went up and down the corridor and quickly disappeared. Maybe that's what Mickey felt."

"Where did you feel it, Holly?"

Abby met the boys as they were following Holly down the corridor. "Hey where are you going, Holly?"

"Oh, Abby, I think I know what happened to Mickey. I felt a cold spot this morning right about here. I don't feel it now, do you, Abby?"

"No, I've never felt it. It may not be the same ghost as the one we had upstairs. Let's go up there and see if we can conjure it up. Are you boys ready?"

"Ah, sure, let's go catch ourselves a ghost," Davey ventured.

Derek chirped in, "I don't think we can actually catch a ghost, can we?" Derek's voice quavered.

"Well, I don't know but we will soon find out, won't we?" Davey added with a smirk showing more bravado than he actually felt.

With Abby and Holly in the lead the group moved slowly up the stairs and down the corridors and in and out of all the rooms. There were four bedrooms, three bathrooms on the second level. Each room did not reveal anything to them.

The boys were disappointed but turned around and headed back downstairs.

"What's in these three rooms, Abby?" Davey inquired.

"Oh, those are rooms we don't use. Two of them are bedrooms and one door leads to the cellar."

"Hmm, Davey, maybe we should check them out too, along with the cellar."

"My dad won't let us go down the cellar. He said it is too dangerous to go there alone. Only he has been down there to store some boxes and other stuff we don't want right now."

"Okay, maybe another time. Thanks, Abby and Holly, for having us over and showing us around. I guess the ghost or ghosts are hiding away. Maybe we can come back at night to see if we have better luck."

"Sure, I'll check with Mom about that. I should tell her what this is about. Can't use the same excuse about homework. Right?" Abby giggled and smiled at Davey.

"No, I guess not. Well, we better get going. Thanks again."

"Oh, and Mrs. Rizzo, thank you for the snacks. They were really good," Davey announced.

Derek piped in, "Yeah, they were delicious!"

"Oh, boys, how nice of you to say. Happy that you enjoyed them. Maybe we will see you both again. Be careful riding your bikes home."

"Yes, Ma'am," the twins chirped in unison.

The girls walked the boys out and Abby said, "Thank you Davey for helping me with my math. I think I understand it better."

Holly turned to Derek and added, "Yes, thank you, Derek, I agree with Abby. I understand it better too. You guys are smart and know your math." Holly winked at Derek and smiled.

"Did you boys hear my mom? She said she wants to see you back here again."

"Yes, I did. That leaves things open for us to come back again to check on the ghosts," Davey added enthusiastically.

"We better go, Davey. It will be getting dark by the time we get home. You heard what Aunt Gigi said."

"Okay, yeah, we better leave. Well, see you girls at school tomorrow. Thanks for inviting us over. Look forward to the next time we visit. Maybe we'll be luckier with catching a glimpse of the ghosts.

CHAPTER FOUR

Sharing Notes with Aunt Gigi

When the twins arrived back at Aunt Gigi's she was at the door waiting for them. She looked at her watch and smiled. "Well, looks like you made it in time. Your mother will be happy to hear that you do listen."

"We try, Aunt Gigi," Davey remarked and smiled.

"Yeah, we do, Aunt Gigi. Even though Mom doesn't agree." Derek pronounced.

"Did you have any luck finding your ghosts at the Sheridan House?" Aunt Gigi watched her nephews' faces for a reaction to her question.

"Well, we didn't, but I think Mickey may have come into contact with one. He rushed out of the house saying he was feeling sick from eating too many snacks."

"Snacks, he had more snacks? He certainly can eat anyone I know under the table. Where does he put it all?

Lucky that he exercises a lot or he would be one heavy kid," Aunt Gigi giggled.

"In fact, we should call him to find out exactly what he saw. Can we call Ca - I mean, Mickey?" Derek asked.

"Of course, you know where the phone is."

"Thanks, Aunt Gigi." Derek headed out to the kitchen and grabbed the phone off the wall.

"We can talk more about it once Derek finds out what Mickey saw. Mickey may be more receptive to spirits than either of you boys are even if he isn't aware of that fact."

Davey and Aunt Gigi sat and waited with not much more to discuss until they had more information.

Derek came bounding back into the living room where Davey and Aunt Gigi were sitting wearing a wide smile on his face.

"Well, what did Mickey say, Derek? You certainly look happy about whatever it is."

"Yeah, whatever, Davey. Listen I was thinking over what Mickey said and, well, you know how he is. He always gives me a chuckle."

Davey tried not to show how anxious he was by his voice. "Derek, come on. Tell us!"

"Oh right, sorry, Bro. He wasn't feeling well about the extra snacks by the way but also he said his stomach became more upset after he had the encounter."

"And…what else, Derek?"

"Okay, okay, I'm getting to it," Derek smirked as he continued, "Mickey said he walked down the corridor and couldn't peek into any of the rooms because all the doors were closed. But when he got to the end of the corridor he noticed a cold breeze crossing in front of him. There was no way the breeze was caused by an open window. Also, he looked up at the walls and said there were photos of old people whose eyes appeared to be following him as he walked along. That's when he decided to hightail it out of there as fast as he could."

"What do you think about all this, Aunt Gigi?" Davey looked at his aunt for some feedback.

"Yeah, what do you think, Aunt Gigi?" Derek added.

"I believe he had an encounter with a ghost. As for the pictures on the wall. That is something altogether different. The pictures each have a ghost locked inside them. We are looking, therefore, at more than one ghost here."

"You're kidding, right, Aunt Gigi?" Derek yelped.

"What did you say - each of those pictures have a ghost locked inside? Davey inquired.

"It appears so, Davey. But not to worry. Once the major ghost is taken care of the others will soon follow. It is his spirit that is the strongest and is keeping the other spirits locked away inside the pictures."

"What can we do to help them get out, Aunt Gigi?" Derek questioned further.

"That is a good question, Derek. We, or should I say you, go there and observe the ghost in his element. Find out what the ghost is doing to get attention. He could be mischievous and playing pranks on the people living there or he could be angry about his manner of death and dangerous. I say he, but it could be a she."

"We plan to go back to Abby's house at night. She said she would get permission from her mother for us to come over another time. I think Mom would be good with that as long as you talk to her about this. It would help us. Would you, Aunt Gigi?" Davey's voice pleaded.

"Ha, I'll do what I can, boys. But listen you could be taking on more than you can handle. If you need me there, please call. Okay? I have handled ghosts before in my day." Aunt Gigi smiled but her face did not show how worried she really was. She had plans to watch over the boys more closely at the Sheridan's House without them knowing.

"Okay, thanks, Aunt Gigi," the twins replied in unison.

The phone rang and Aunt Gigi left to answer it while the boys used "TT" to discuss the news about multiple ghosts.

I can't believe it, Davey! There are multiple ghosts now to deal with. What are we going to do?

I guess we will find out once we get back there and commune with them.

Commune with them? What are you crazy? I don't want to commune with them. I only want to get them to leave town, skedaddle. Know what I mean?

Yeah, I know. You're using another one of Dad's words. I don't particularly want to encounter this ghost either. He sounds like he could be a strong presence if he is containing so many other ghosts in the house. Creepy, if you ask me!

Aunt Gigi came back in and waited for the boys to stop using "TT" to announce, "Boys that was your mother. She's home and wants you there pronto. Be careful."

"Okay, let's go, Derek. See you tomorrow, Aunt Gigi."

"Thanks for the help, Aunt Gigi. See you later," Derek added.

"Yeah, thanks for everything, Aunt Gigi," Davey agreed.

The boys raced home sharing "TT" all the way. That was the good thing about "TT". It could be done anywhere.

We have a lot to think about when we go to Abby's again. Where should we begin, Davey?

I think we ought to go with the flow, Bro. Wait and see what the ghost does first. We may not even come into contact with it. I hope it's a guy.

What difference does that make, Davey? It's only a spirit after all. It doesn't have a body.

I guess you're right. Do you think we will actually see it or feel it like Mickey did?

Who knows, Davey? We'll be ready for whatever happens, won't we?

We will be. We can do it together, Derek, like we did with all the other cases so far.

It's kind of exciting to think we will go head to head with a ghost.

Yeah, who would believe it?

The boys argued over who reached the garage first to put away his bike.

"Aw come on, Davey! You revved up your bike again, didn't you?"

"Ha, I will never tell!"

"Boys, quite the fighting and take Aggy out. She has been waiting a long time. I have my hands full and couldn't let her out yet."

"Sure Mom! Hi Aggy, how are you girl? Yeah we missed you too!"

A lot of barking and jumping up and down was done by a happy dog as the boys grabbed Aggy's leash and headed back outside to play.

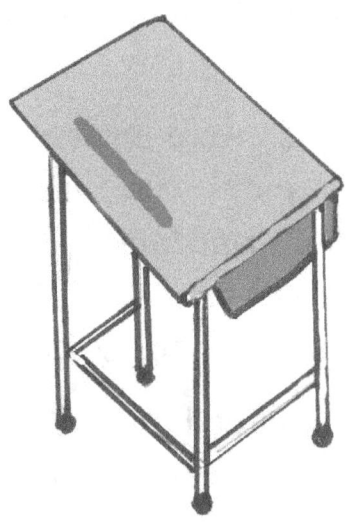

CHAPTER FIVE

School Gets in the Way

Mrs. Trakko droned on and on about a reading assignment as the boys used "TT" to discuss their new case. They didn't look at each other and stared straight ahead in order to look like they were interested in what the teacher was discussing.

When the twins were involved in their twin speak they were unaware of anything else happening. Their eyes glazed over and their faces took on a funny expression of amusement.

Mrs. Trakko turned toward the class and took note of the twins' expressions. She walked down the aisle and came to their seats which were one behind the other, Davey being in the front seat.

Mrs. Trakko looked at Davey but he did not look back at her. She tapped his shoulder and he jumped and met her eyes with a surprised look, all amusement now gone.

Oh-oh, Davey. You are in deep trouble!

Shush, Derek. You are next!

Mrs. Trakko leaned closer to Davey and whispered, "Is there a problem here Mr. Donato? Would you like to share your amusement about my lesson?"

"Um, no Ma'am. I wasn't amused at all."

Derek guffawed at his brother's remark.

"Do you want to share something, Mr. Donato?" Mrs. Trakko addressed Derek.

"Oh no, Ma'am. I have nothing to share." Derek tried to keep his smirk at bay.

"It seems you still think something is funny. Maybe you both would like to spend some time after school in detention and explain what is so amusing."

"Oh no, Ma'am. We're fine. We have nothing to share. We really enjoyed your discussion. You had a great delivery," Derek stated.

"Yes, Ma'am. We love Reading and your class rocks," Davey said trying to smooth things out with the teacher.

"Hmm, well, try to look more interested, boys. I will be keeping an eye on both of you and will expect to call on you to answer questions. Do you think you can stay awake and alert enough to answer them?"

"Oh yes, Mrs. Trakko. We will," Derek responded.

"Let's see that you do. Class, let's get back to our discussion about the new book I expect you to read this month. We will have a test on the subject matter to see how well you are retaining what you read."

Mrs. Trakko went back to her desk and continued to drone on. But this time the boys kept serious expressions on their faces as they listened.

Once out of the classroom the boys sighed in relief. "Wow that was close. We can't afford detention. Mom would never let us go to Abby's house," Davey stressed.

"Oh boy, that's for sure, Derek. We had better work on our expressions when we use "TT". I never knew we looked amused when we used it. Did you"?

"No, why would I know that? I don't look in the mirror or even at you when we use twin-speak."

"I guess we should look in the mirror or at least at each other so we can practice putting on serious expressions," Derek added.

"Yeah, that could work. Hey, Davey, let's get our homework done early when we get home and afterwards ask Mom about going to Abby's again."

"Sure, but Abby has got to tell us when her mother says we can go."

"Yeah, I know that, but we can prepare Mom for that ahead of time. We can share our findings with her too."

"You are getting wilier all the time, Derek."

The boys finished their homework in record time and went to the kitchen to find their mother.

"Hi Mom. What's for dinner?" Davey inquired.

"Spaghetti and meatballs. Sound good?"

"Oh yeah! My favorite!" Derek jumped in with enthusiasm.

"Happy to hear it." Dinner will be in half an hour boys. Go get cleaned up."

"Um, Mom, can we ask you something?" Davey moved closer as his mother turned toward him.

"What's wrong, Davey?"

"Nothing really, but we want to share our new case with you."

"New case?" Laura stopped stirring the sauce and took a seat at the table as she waved the boys over.

Once they were seated Derek picked up the discussion, "Mom, we met two girls in school today and Aunt Gigi let us go to their house. They bought the Sheridan House."

"Hmm, I see. Aunt Gigi did call me about that. She checked with me about allowing you to go to their house. I agreed. Did you find any ghosts?"

"Well, we didn't but Mickey did."

"Well, Derek, he didn't actually see a ghost but rather felt the presence of one."

"Yeah, but at least he felt something. We didn't experience anything. That's why we wanted to ask you if we could go back there again. Mrs. Rizzo said she hoped to see us again."

"Mrs. Rizzo? Is that the mother of these two girls?"

"No, she is Abby's mother. Holly is Abby's cousin. She's staying there until her parents come back from a trip overseas," Davey explained.

"As long as you are respectful while you are there to everyone. When are you planning to go back there?"

"Of course, Mom, we are always respectful of others. That's the reason Mrs. Rizzo wants us to come back. She liked us," Derek stated.

"We ought to call Abby and see when we can come back as long as you give us the okay," Davey continued with a smile on his face.

"Okay, you can go back. But I still want you home before dark. You know I don't like you riding your bikes at that time. It's too dangerous."

"Thanks Mom. We promise to be back before dark," Derek responded with a wink and added, "can we bring Aggy over to Aunt Gigi's? She wants to see her."

"Okay, but what are you going to do with Aggy when you go over to Abby's house?"

"Aggy can stay with Aunt Gigi. She would love to visit with her 'Aggy girl.' That's what Aunt Gigi called her," Davey chuckled.

"Okay, just this once. We don't want to take advantage of Aunt Gigi. Please get cleaned up and set the table for me."

"Sure thing, Mom, thanks!" The boys yipped and ran off to wash their hands.

"TT" was shared as the boys set the table.

Nice going, Derek, telling Mom that we were courteous and that is why Mrs. Rizzo wants us back.

Yeah, I thought that was a nice touch.

Politeness always gets us in the door. You know that.

Yeah, Derek, I guess you're right.

Besides I'm looking forward to seeing Abby again.

Me too, no, I mean I look forward to seeing Holly again. She has pretty hair.

Oh, I think you are smitten, little brother!

Um, maybe a little. But don't tell anyone or I will...

Same goes for me about Abby. Let's keep this girl stuff under our hats especially from the girls.

I agree, Bro!

I'll call Abby after dinner. We can plan together when we can go back. We have some ghosts to capture.

Capture? You mean you want to capture them?

Ha, not literally, Derek.

Can't we scoot them out of the house?

How do we scoot anything?

Oh, I don't know. Let me think about it.

Dinner's ready. Let's eat! Talk later.

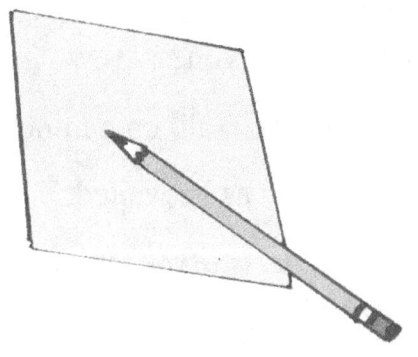

CHAPTER SIX

Preparations Underway

Davey dialed Abby's number and waited. He was surprised when Abby answered instead of her mother.

"Hello."

"Abby? Hi, this is Davey."

"Hi Davey."

"My mother said we can come over. When would be good for you?"

"I'll ask my mom. Hold on a minute."

Davey used "TT" as he waited.

Abby's asking her mother. Keep your fingers crossed, Derek.

"Davey, she said today would be fine. I had to tell her about the ghosts and that you are junior detectives. She actually told me that she felt something too."

"Really? Wow, that's cool. It's our time to experience it."

"What time can you come over, Davey?"

"We can come over after school once we check in with Aunt Gigi. She worries if we don't. She takes her job seriously as our protector. We don't have a sitter but we have a protector. She keeps us out of trouble."

"Ha, that's funny, Davey. You have a great sense of humor."

"Oh, um, thanks, Abby."

"See you at school tomorrow and afterward too."

"Look forward to it, Davey."

"Yeah, okay. Thanks, Abby."

Davey hung up the phone, his face a rosy pink, which Derek noticed.

"Don't say a thing, Derek!"

"Oh, I wasn't going to say a thing, Bro," Derek smirked.

"So, are we all set to go tomorrow?"

"Yep, Abby said it's a go. Oh, she also told me that her mother said she felt a presence too."

"Really? That's cool. Maybe we will feel something tomorrow too."

***

School dragged on as the boys kept looking at the clock in each class. When it was time for lunch the girls came over right away and sat next to the twins much to their delight.

"Hi girls." Davey smiled as he made room for them at the table.

"Hi Davey and Derek," Abby and Holly reacted together.

Derek smiled and went back to eating his lunch.

"What are you guys planning for today at my house? Do you have any special tactics in mind?" Abby asked in between bites of her sandwich.

"Not really, Abby. We go along with the flow and make things up as we go," Davey rhymed.

"You are clever, Davey," Abby crooned.

"Oh boy!" Derek guffawed.

Davey gave his brother a warning look behind Abby's back.

Using "TT", Derek responded in kind.

I got your eerie eyeball, Bro! Ha!

After lunch Davey planned to peruse a few books on ghosts while in Media along with checking the internet for info. He wanted to take some notes and talk things over with Derek before they went to Abby's. He did like to plan ahead even though he had told Abby differently.

Holly talked to Derek during this time non-stop while he shoveled in his lunch. She didn't seem to mind that he was not giving her all his attention.

Derek was enjoying hearing Holly's voice and would mumble a response in between bites. He exchanged a few smiles with her too that made her happy even if he didn't say much.

Once the bell rang the group was ready to head back to their last few classes. They waved goodbye as they left the café.

In Media Davey and Derek picked out a few books and took notes in preparation for their ghost hunt.

One book mentioned ghost hunters use a variety of techniques and tools such as an EMF (electromagnetic fields) meter for cold spots, digital video cameras, and audio recorder to capture any unexplained noises.

Derek read through all the hype about belief statistics and skepticism involving paranormal activity. He still did not know what to think about all this or what he would do if he did feel or see a presence.

Derek, what do you think about all this stuff? It sounds too crazy to believe, don't you think?

I don't know Davey. But I guess we will find out one way or the other soon. Maybe today we'll see something.

I hope so, Bro.

We can go over our notes on the bus and let Cat know about going over to Abby's again. That is, if he's game. He might not be.

Yeah, you are right. He might be too spooked to come with us, Davey.

There goes the bell. One more class to go.

Yeah, it seems like this day is dragging.

We only need to get through Mr. Colton's class and we will be home free, and soon you will see Abby.

Yeah, and you will see Holly!

The twins gathered up the books and returned them to the teacher and took their notes with them to their next class.

Mr. Colton gave out tons more homework and promised a test the next day. The boys knew they had to get their homework done before they went to Abby's house. They planned to do some on the bus in between talking to Cat about going to Abby's.

Cat was already on the bus by the time the twins hopped on. They sat next to him and began to explain what they were going to do.

"I don't know if my mom will let me go again. She expects me to watch my sister today while she goes grocery shopping."

"It's okay, Cat, if you don't want to go because of the presence. It would have shaken me too," Derek stated trying to make Cat feel better.

"No, it's not like that. I was sick to my stomach from the extra snacks, that's all. I wasn't frightened by it, not really. Maybe surprised. I'll go back another time. Okay?"

"No problem, Cat. We'll fill you in whether something happens or not," Davey reiterated.

"Well, it's our stop. Talk to you later, Cat." Derek waved and ran down the steps.

The twins unlocked the garage, let Aggy out for a quick trip around the yard and invited her to go along with them as they grabbed their bikes and headed over to Aunt Gigi's.

Aunt Gigi was doing her own preparations to help the boys with their new case. She feared that they could be in danger if this ghost was more than mischievous.

"Hi boys. Come on in. Snacks are ready. Oh, you brought my Aggy girl! How are you girl? Looking so good, you are! Come on out and get yourself a tasty snack too!" Aunt Gigi opened her arms as the boys dashed under them, artfully avoiding her huge hugs, and headed to the kitchen.

Aunt Gigi chuckled and set out cold glasses of milk for the boys as she sat next to them with a cup of tea and Aggy at her feet happily chomping on some milk bones.

"Well, how was your day at school, boys? Do you have homework?"

"Okay, almost done with our homework. Did some on the bus."

"Good to know, Davey. Anything else to share?" Aunt Gigi was trying to pull out more information as the boys ate.

"Mom said we can go over to the Sheridan House again today. We will finish up our homework first and head over there. Okay?" Derek looked up from his snacks to look at Aunt Gigi.

"No problem. Your mom already called to tell me. I was wondering when you were going to mention it."

"Oh, sorry, Aunt Gigi. We were going to tell you," Davey apologized.

"All forgiven, boys, not to worry. I wanted to discuss your next trip to the Sheridan House. I have some suggestions for you."

"Really? We have some stuff that we looked up today to share with you too about ghost hunting."

"I see, you are quite impressive as detectives, Derek."

"Derek, let Aunt Gigi talk. We need all the help that we can get."

"Sorry Aunt Gigi. Oh, can Aggy stay with you while we are at Abby's house?"

"That's all right, Derek. Yes, I would love to have Aggy stay and visit with me. What I want to share with you is, I have experience with ghosts from many years back. I have something that I think would be helpful to you." Aunt Gigi pulled a medium-sized device from the pocket of her sweater that looked like a flashlight.

"What is that, Aunt Gigi?" Davey enquired.

"This, dear boys, is what I call a ghost flasher. It has been used in our family for generations to uncover spirits. It will reveal a presence and help to contain it. It will also protect you from any mischief or harm that the apparition may try to inflict upon you."

"Wow that sounds better than what we saw online or in the books at school. How does it work?" Derek asked in an enthusiastic tone.

Aunt Gigi stood up and extended the ghost flasher to the boys. Davey took it and examined it as Derek peeked over his shoulder for a closer look.

"Do you see this red button? That is the one you press when you see or feel a presence. Once you focus onto the presence you press the yellow button here which will contain the presence."

"Contain it? Do you mean capture it inside this device?" Davey asked clearly excited over this prospect.

"Yes, it will contain it but you must take it away from the house. Once you leave the house you can let it go. It will not survive outside the house and will disappear to the other side. But the only catch is, you have to contain the major ghost. This one will bring all the other ghosts with him. If you don't get him or her successfully he will become stronger and you will not be able to use this device again on him.

"Oh, boy, how will we know if we got him, Aunt Gigi?"

"You will know, Derek, by the color of the tube. It will glow blue. The deeper the blue the more ghosts you have captured."

"Do you expect there to be many ghosts in Sheridan House?" Davey asked in a quivering voice.

"Yes, I believe there are many ghosts there. The one that is the strongest is holding them at bay. It is not going to be an easy task. I will watch over you from afar through Mianna (Aunt Gigi's faithful cat inside her crystal ball). She always comes through for me. All you boys are required to do is open your minds to me and I will be able to guide you."

"How do we open our minds to you, Aunt Gigi?" Derek queried.

"You think of me and your mind will be opened and receptive to Mianna."

"Okay, we can do that, huh, Davey?"

"Yes, we can."

"Okay, boys. Let's get this table cleared off so you can finish your homework and go a-hunting." Aunt Gigi giggled clearly amused with her own humor.

As the boys headed out Aunt Gigi warned, "Take care, boys. If you require my help, keep your minds open. Aggy and I will be here waiting for you."

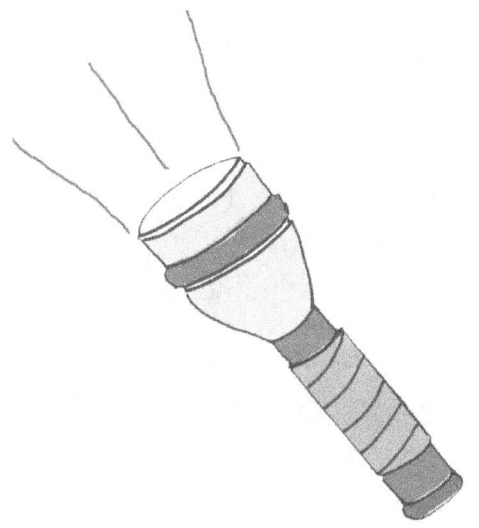

CHAPTER SEVEN

The Hunt Begins

Davey and Derek raced over to Abby's house and pulled up to her front door parking their bikes alongside the walkway.

The girls were at the front door before the boys got to the top step. Smiles were shared as the boys were welcomed in.

Mrs. Rizzo called out, "Welcome boys. Please come in. Where's your friend, Mickey?"

"Oh, he couldn't come. He had to watch his sister while his mother went shopping. He said he would come another time though."

"I hope so. He was such a nice young man, so well-bred. Please go wash up. I have some snacks for you and the girls. Same place as last time."

The boys raced off to the bathroom to clean up and hurried back to the kitchen. The girls were already there waiting for them.

The snacks were even better this time. Even though the twins already had a snack at their aunt's they dug into the dips and chips with gusto.

Mrs. Rizzo loved watching them and commented, "It's so nice to see you enjoying my snacks."

"They are delicious, Mrs. Rizzo. Thank you so much!" Davey wiped his mouth as he said this.

"Yes, thank you, Mrs. Rizzo. Your snacks rock!" Derek added for emphasis.

"Thank you, boys. You are so polite. I like to see that. Too many youngsters today do not know simple courtesies as 'please and thank you.' Your parents are proud of you, I'm sure."

"Yes, ma'am." The twins replied in unison.

"Abby tells me that you are junior detectives and have solved other cases. Do you think you can solve the case of our ghost?"

"We hope we can, Mrs. Rizzo," Davey responded trying to sound confident.

"We'll do our best, Ma'am," Derek added as he winked at Holly.

Holly smiled in response as she blushed an attractive shade of rosy pink which Derek noticed with pleasure.

"I think you boys will do your best. I have confidence in you. All I ask is that you be careful. I don't know if this ghost is dangerous. Do your parents mind you doing this?"

"Thank you, Mrs. Rizzo," Davey replied and continued, "Our parents aren't worried about us. They know we can take care of ourselves."

"Well, I'm relieved that they trust you to do things like this and not worry."

"They probably worry anyway though," Derek added with a smile.

"Yeah, you are probably right. I know I worry about Abby and Holly all the time. I will worry about you two while you are here. Please be careful boys, okay?"

"Yes, we will, Mrs. Rizzo," Davey and Derek agreed.

Abby began cleaning up the table and leftover snacks along with Holly's help. The girls were anxious and whispered to one and another, "What do you think the boys are going to do to find the ghost?"

"I don't know, Holly. I'm a little frightened to meet a ghost. I have only felt the cold draft but never saw the actual ghost, have you?"

"Well, not really. What does a ghost look like anyway?"

"Wait a minute, Abby. Did you think you saw it?"

"Um, I did see something in the room with all the books, the den. It was a shadowy thing that came from the shelves as I was looking for a book to read two nights ago. When I looked up again it was gone. It could have been my imagination though."

"Oh, I'm glad I didn't see it. It would have creeped me out. You should tell the boys. They need to know where to look."

"Yeah, I guess you are right, Holly. I will. Let's get these dishes cleaned up so we can get a move on and go hunting," Abby giggled nervously.

The boys were doing their "TT" as they waited for the girls to finish cleaning up the kitchen.

Davey, look over there. Do you see that?

What? What did you see?

Oh, it's gone now. It was a wispy white cloud of a thing that drifted down the hallway heading toward the room at the end.

Let's go ask the girls what's in that room. It could be where the ghost lives or haunts so to speak.

Derek, did you bring the ghost flasher? I don't have it. We could really use it.

No, I don't have it either. I think Aunt Gigi took it and forgot to give it back to us.

The girls stood a few feet away from the boys and observed the smirks on their faces as they seemed to be in a trance.

"Hey, Davey? Are you with this world?" Abby queried.

Davey whipped his head around and looked at Abby. "Oh, sorry, Abby. I was deep in thought trying to come up with a plan to find this ghost."

Holly edged closer to Derek until she was nearly shoulder to shoulder with him. She met his eyes and said, "Is everything okay, Derek? You both look like you were somewhere else. Did you see something?"

Derek looked over at Davey and nodded, "Well, Davey, you should tell them."

"Yeah, I did see something. It was a white wispy thing traveling down the corridor. It disappeared into the room at the end."

"Ooh, Abby that could be what you saw," Holly exclaimed as her eyes widened in surprise.

"You saw it, Abby?" Davey asked excitement in his voice.

"I was telling Holly how I saw something a couple of nights ago in the den. I guess it was a library at one time because it has floor to ceiling shelves with old books. We use it as a den to sit, read, do our homework or watch TV. Dad wants to tear down all the shelves but I won't let him. The books are old and have some history there."

Holly added, "Maybe that's where the ghost lives, in the old books or behind the shelves."

Derek nodded in agreement. "You may be right, Holly. There could be something to that."

Davey suggested, "Why don't we go to the den and check it out. Maybe we'll get lucky."

The girls led the way and stopped at the doorway peeking in cautiously.

The twins walked around the girls into the large room and looked over at the book shelves that reached up to the fifty foot ceilings. Along one wall was a ladder that was attached to a track that allowed it to roll along the shelves enabling the reader to access books much easier at all heights.

Running his hands along the edges of the shelves Davey looked for any openings. Derek climbed up the ladder and began to roll along vicariously for Holly's attention.

Holly chuckled clearly amused as Derek rolled back and forth until Davey hollered to get his attention.

"Derek, stop! Come here, look at this!"

Abby rushed over to where Davey was standing at the corner of the room near the doorway.

"What? What's wrong, Davey?" Derek jumped down the last two steps of the ladder and made a big landing to get Holly's attention once again.

"What is it, Davey?" Abby peeked around Davey's shoulder.

Derek, with Holly close behind, looked at the edge of the shelving that Davey was pointing to.

"What is that, Davey?"

"I'm not quite sure, but it could be…"

"Oh, look at this!" Davey exclaimed with disbelief evident in his voice.

"Wow, it looks like it's a doorway," Derek shouted but lowered his voice as not to alert Mrs. Rizzo to their find.

The girls couldn't contain their enthusiasm as they giggled nervously and helped the boys pull the edge of the shelf away from the wall.

"What's in there?" Abby asked?

"I can't see. It's too dark. Do you have a flashlight, Abby?"

"Sure, wait a minute." Abby raced out into the kitchen and came back in a few seconds with a large flashlight.

"Wow that is a big flashlight, Abby. We could see the length of the Empire State Building with this one!" Davey said as he took it from her and turned it on.

Derek and the girls pushed forward to look inside the secret room. Who knew how long this room was there and what secrets it held. It could have treasure or maybe something that the original owners wanted to hide.

What Davey saw surprised and delighted him at the same time. This really was going to be a fun adventure no matter what happened.

CHAPTER EIGHT

The Secret Passageways

Derek was right behind Davey as they entered the room illuminated by the large flashlight.

The opening was as large as the shelf that hid it and it had two passageways, one to the left and the other to the right. As the boys turned the flashlight to the first passageway they saw a door. Both passageways were not very wide but at the end of each was a door.

They moved as one with the girls staying right on the boys' heels for fear of something jumping out at them. They ducked under cobwebs so thick that they held their breaths so as not to breathe them in.

"Wait, Davey. We shouldn't go too far. We may get lost in here," Derek voiced his apprehension,

"Oh yeah, Davey," Abby cried as her level of fear rose and gave her goosebumps.

"I think we should go back," Holly exclaimed in a shaky voice.

"Okay girls. Why don't you go back to the den and wait for us. We will go check one door and come right back. All right? We'll be fine, right Derek?"

"Um, yeah sure, Davey." Trembling and hanging onto his brother, Derek nodded in agreement. "We'll be fine, girls."

The girls rushed out of the room and went back to the den and waited for the boys to finish up their search of the first door.

Derek moved slowly behind Davey and used "TT" so the girls would not hear them.

Where do you think this first doorway goes, Davey?

I guess it will take us to another part of the house. There must be secret doors in the walls in several rooms to match these doorways.

That would make sense, Davey. As long as we don't get lost.

We won't get lost, Derek. If we go through this door we will end up in another room. We can come through that room and get back here, no problem.

Okay, if you say so. We could yell for the girls and they would guide us back to the den with their voices.

The twins kept walking and opened the door and steered the light up and down another corridor. This didn't look good. Where would they go? The walkway appeared to be going uphill.

"Davey, there's another door. Maybe we should go back now."

"No Derek, hang in there a little longer. Look, at the wall over here. There is a little light coming from behind it. Help me push against this wall. There has to be another secret door in the wall to get into the room here."

The boys pushed with their hands and shoulders as the wall abruptly gave way and they ended up on the floor of a bedroom. Looking around they noticed it was one of the girl's rooms by the display of posters and girly stuff.

Closing the doorway in the wall the boys headed out of the room and made their way back downstairs to the den where the girls were sitting whispering nervously with their heads together. They jumped up in surprise as the boys came into the den.

"Where did you end up, Davey? Are you okay?" Abby ran over to Davey and touched his arm to make sure he was unharmed.

"Oh, I think we ended up in either your room or Holly's. It's the one with the pink and purple bedspread.

"That's mine," Abby announced.

"You mean to say that the first door on the left went to my bedroom?"

"Well, not directly. The door took us to another corridor with a second door at the end. But we didn't take the other door. Instead we noticed a light coming from under the wall near the first door and pushed against it. It opened after a little while and we ended up in your room."

"I bet the second door at the end of that corridor goes to another bedroom, maybe Holly's," Derek surmised.

"Wow that is cool!" Holly announced surprised at her reaction for the whole secret passageway frightened her. She added, "What if someone gets into the corridors and sneaks into our rooms at night?"

Abby noticed Holly's face was pale and her hands were shaking. Abby grabbed hold of Holly's hand and pressed it to give her some support and said, "It's okay, Holly. Don't worry. No one knows about these corridors but us."

"What do you think they used these corridors for, Davey?" Abby questioned.

"Why don't we look up the house online and see what we can find. Maybe there is some mention of what this house was used for. Also, the secret passageways might show up on the floor plan."

Abby went to pick up her father's laptop off the desk nearby and brought it back to the group. She placed it on Davey's lap in invitation. "This is my Dad's laptop but he lets us use it."

"Thanks, Abby. Okay, let's see what we can find."

Davey used a search engine that Abby's father had on his laptop and found the Sheridan House with several hits. One hit mentioned the house had been used when it was first built over one hundred years ago as an old-fashioned version of a bed and breakfast. It could hold ten to twelve visitors at a time. Beds were put in all the rooms when necessary, short of the kitchen.

Derek looked at another hit and it said that there were secret passageways that were used to sneak visitors who were notorious or infamous in and out of the house under cover. It was alleged that the passageways may have been used by these notorious visitors to steal from the people who stayed and slept here.

"Does it say anything about ghosts inhabiting the house and passageways?" Abby inquired not sure she really wanted to know the answer.

"Well, let's see," Derek continued perusing the site. "No, it doesn't, but wait. Let's look up ghosts in the Sheridan House and see what comes up."

Derek's fingers flew across the keyboard as a dozen hits came up about ghosts. The boys read through all of them.

Davey began to explain, "It does say here that some of the visitors did experience some strange occurrences like cold spots, white smoke drifting around the room, lights going on and off and unexplained noises, and things disappearing from their rooms."

Derek looked over at Davey and used "TT" quickly.

Should we tell them what Aunt Gigi told us about Mrs. Sheridan and how she died here?

No, absolutely not! They are frightened enough already about these passageways.

Okay, but we should tell them eventually.

Well, we will wait until we need to do that. I don't see how knowing that will help them.

Okay, I guess you're right, Davey.

Shush, Derek, the girls are looking at us.

Abby watched the twins' expression as they seemed to be far away once again. She was puzzled as she spoke up, "Davey, is everything all right?"

"Oh yeah, everything's fine. No problems here. I think we read enough about the house for now, don't you?"

"Yeah, I think we know a lot more than we did before. What are we going to do next?" Holly enquired.

"Well, I think we have done enough for today. We have to get home before it gets dark, our mother's orders."

"Okay, we know what you mean, Derek. We get into trouble if we don't get in before dark too. I don't know what Aunt Jane thinks would happen to us if we stayed out a minute after dark?" Holly said as she smiled at Derek.

"Yeah, I don't know either. Well, it's time for us to leave. Thanks for having us over again, girls," Davey said.

Derek nodded to Holly and went out to the kitchen to find Mrs. Rizzo and extend his thanks to her too.

Mrs. Rizzo walked the boys to the door along with the girls and said, "You are welcome, boys. Did you find anything of interest about our ghost?"

Abby interrupted and said, "Not really, Mom. But the boys will come back again to keep looking around. Is that okay with you?"

"Yes, of course. It would be a pleasure to have you over again. Maybe we can have your whole family over for dinner one night. I will call your mother and set something up. Abby has your number. You can see the house after dark. The ghost may make an appearance at night."

"Oh, that would be great, Mrs. Rizzo. I bet we will see the ghost." Davey and Derek said in unison with excitement in their voices.

Mrs. Rizzo chuckled. "Do you boys always talk at the same time like that?"

"I guess so," the twins announced as they, too, laughed.

Mrs. Rizzo walked away and let the girls say their goodbyes to the twins.

Davey whispered to Abby, "Why didn't you tell your mother about what we found?"

"Oh, I wanted to keep that secret for a little longer. We can use them one day when we want to sneak out of our rooms."

"You want to travel those passageways by yourselves?"

"Well, maybe not," Abby giggled and Holly joined her.

"See you girls tomorrow at school," the twins chirped as they headed down the stairs to get their bikes.

The boys raced back to Aunt Gigi's to fill her in about their exciting findings at the Sheridan House. They wanted to ask her a few more questions about Mr. and Mrs. Sheridan too.

Aunt Gigi was waiting at the front window with Aggy as the boys jumped off their bikes and ran up her back stairs.

Aunt Gigi opened the door suddenly and grabbed the boys in an iron-clad hug surprising and shocking them.

"Oh, how are you boys doing? Ha, I got you this time!" Aunt Gigi laughed heartily as she finally released the boys. Aggy saw her chance and jumped on the boys and added her sloppy kisses. The twins patted Aggy and rubbed her head in greeting.

Davey shook his head to clear it and looked at Derek in disbelief.

What happened, Derek?

Our reflexes are getting slow or Aunt Gigi is getting faster for some unexplained reason. She sure is strong for her age!

Yeah, I agree about her strength but I don't believe that she is getting faster. We had our minds on the passageways we found. That was exciting, don't you think?

Oh, yes! Let's tell Aunt Gigi and see what she has to say about them.

Aunt Gigi waited patiently for the boys to finish up their discussion inside their heads.

The boys sat down on the couch next to Aunt Gigi and explained what transpired on their new case.

She nodded and listened and frowned a little when the boys said they had gone into the secret room on their own.

"What do you think, Aunt Gigi?" Derek asked while he held his breath.

"Hmm, very interesting, boys. I do remember there were passageways but thought when the house was sold that they were closed off. Do the Rizzo's know about them?"

"No, they don't and Abby didn't let us tell her mother about them. Which I thought was kind of strange since she was too afraid to go very far into the passageway with us," Derek stressed.

"Yes, I agree. That is strange. She may have her reasons. Maybe she and Holly want to explore them on their own."

"Oh no, they were scared! I saw their faces, Aunt Gigi," Davey added and asked his first question. "Do you believe that the ghosts are hiding inside the passageways?"

"That is possible. They can get to each room quicker by traveling unseen through them. Maybe that is why you haven't seen them yet."

Derek continued by saying, "Well, Mrs. Rizzo wants us to go over one night for dinner with our family. She said we can do more exploring for ghosts too."

"Well, there's a good chance that you could see a ghost at night. They do have a tendency of coming out at night. That is when you will use the ghost flasher."

Uncle George appeared at the doorway to the living room and said, "Hi boys. How are you doing?"

"Great, Uncle George. How are you?" Davey said in greeting.

"Not bad for an old man," he chuckled and turning to Aunt Gigi, asked, "What's for dinner, dear?"

"The boys are leaving, George, and I will be cooking soon. Why don't you get yourself a cup of coffee and read the paper and relax." Aunt Gigi smiled and nodded at him.

"Well, boys. You better get on home. Your mother will be calling soon."

"Okay, Aunt Gigi. Let's go, Derek."

"See you tomorrow afternoon, Aunt Gigi," Davey said as he ducked under her arms and ran for the door with Derek and Aggy close on his heels

Aunt Gigi giggled after the boys and sighed, "Oh these boys are such a joy!"

She had to keep them safe. She knew how headstrong and fearless they could be. There was more to these ghosts than the boys knew. Maybe it was time to dust off the ghost flasher and visit with Mianna.

CHAPTER NINE

A Mischievous Ghost

The twins collated their notes and sat back on Davey's bed and evaluated their findings. Aggy slept on the floor nearby but kept her ears alert in case the boys wanted to take her out to play.

"Well, what do you think about this so far, Derek?" Davey reached over and ruffled Aggy's fur as she sighed contentedly.

"I think we are on the verge of seeing the major ghost but we ought to ask Aunt Gigi for the ghost flasher. What if we actually encounter it without the flasher? What will happen?"

"I...I don't know, Derek. We better ask Aunt Gigi for the tool. But...I'm afraid that we may be over our heads in this one."

"I don't know about that yet. I think Aunt Gigi is right that there is more than one ghost here. Why did Abby want to keep the passageways a secret from her mother?"

"Maybe she plans to use them to hide stuff from her parents or...I don't really know. She was frightened about going in there with us. I doubt she will enter them on her own."

***

Over at the Sheridan House, Abby and Holly opened the secret passage and peeked in using the large flashlight again.

"What are you doing, Abby? I thought you didn't want to go in there alone?"

"I'm not alone. I have you with me, Holly. I'm not as nervous as I was before. After all the boys went in and nothing bothered them and they came back unharmed. I have a funny feeling that there is something hidden here."

"Do you remember last week when I couldn't find my hairbrush? It suddenly appeared on the floor by the wall next to my bed?"

"Yes, I remember you mentioned that to me. Why? What has that got to do with the passageway?"

"Well, I think we may have a mischievous ghost that moves things at will."

"But maybe you dropped it there and forgot."

"No, that is not the only thing that was moved. In fact, my red and blue scarf is missing and so are my blue socks that I wore yesterday."

"Oh, I better check my room to see if anything is missing there too." Holly ran along to do that before Abby could continue to explain.

"Wait, Holly, where are you going?" Abby sighed, closed the shelf, sat on the couch and waited for Holly to come back. She suddenly wasn't feeling very brave to go in there alone.

Holly ran into her room and searched around through her stuff to verify that there was nothing missing. But when she came to her desk she noticed that her notepad had been moved and her favorite pen was missing. Also, she had left an old book from the shelves on the night table to read tonight but it was not there and her pillow was on the floor.

Holly ran back to the den to report these findings to Abby. When she arrived Abby was sitting on the couch looking at a large book.

"Abby, someone has been in my room! I have stuff that's missing and other stuff that has been moved. Do you think it's the ghost?" Holly asked in a shaky voice.

"Well, either we have someone who is trying to scare us or it's the ghost. Maybe we should tell my mother about this."

"I agree, let's go." Holly hurried out of the den and headed for the kitchen right behind Abby.

"Hey Mom, do you have a minute? Holly and I would like to discuss something with you."

"Sure honey, what is it? Any problem at school?" Mrs. Rizzo held her breath hoping it was nothing to do with boys.

"No, Mom, it's...well, Holly and I found some stuff in our room that was either moved or missing altogether. We're not sure who could have done that. Do you think it's the ghost?"

"Oh my, I never heard of ghosts being able to actually touch physical things and move them. But I don't know very much about ghosts other than what I have read or seen on TV. Let's not worry about this stuff. Maybe you two have been preoccupied with this ghost hunting and forgot where you put your stuff. I'm sure these things will show up or you will remember where they are. Let's not get too crazy about this ghost stuff. Okay honey?" Mrs. Rizzo smiled trying to allay the girls' fears but at the same time trying to relax her own unspoken ones.

"Um Okay, Mom. You may be right." Abby looked over at Holly and shrugged her shoulders.

"Do you girls have any homework to keep you busy?"

"No, we finished it already, Mom." Turning toward Holly, Abby said, "Hey Holly, let's go find some interesting stuff to read in the den." Abby rolled her eyes in that direction.

The girls went back to the den to continue their search. Now they had something to actually search for, their missing items.

With their trusty enormous flashlight lighting the whole area, the girls walked into the passageway and headed to the left where the boys said the secret door was to their rooms. The walkway here rose up, gradually, as they moved along to the second floor.

Abby walked slowly and cautiously afraid to trip with Holly hanging onto her left arm in fear.

"Holly, please don't push me."

Abby screamed as she turned to look at Holly but Holly wasn't where she thought she should be. Who was holding onto her arm if it wasn't Holly?

"I wasn't pushing you. I was walking along with you but not close enough to push you."

"What's wrong, Abby? I'm right here next to you. What you are looking at? What frightened you?"

"Oh, I thought you were hanging onto my left arm and pushing me. But if it wasn't you, who was it?" Abby shivered and waited for Holly to come next to her.

Abby grabbed onto Holly's hand and pulled her closer for comfort.

"It's okay, Abby. I'm right here. I couldn't see anything behind you because I was walking on your right side. Are you sure you want to continue on? We can do this with the boys' help another time." Holly's voice was shaky too.

"No, we got this far, let's continue. There's the door up ahead. The boys said that the area they pushed on was right next to this door. Look for something with spaces for an opening. Here Holly, push here."

The girls pushed and bumped their shoulders into the area that looked like it could be a doorway in the wall. It finally opened and the girls found themselves in Abby's room.

"Wow, look at this! This is cool but definitely creepy! I don't like the idea that someone or something can come into our room when we are sleeping. Maybe we should nail this doorway shut and the one to your room too, Holly. We ought to go back into the corridor and find the one to your room so we can do that or we can go to your room and check the walls for an opening."

"Oh, I don't know if I want to go back in there, Abby. Can I sleep in your room tonight after we nail this door shut?"

"Sure, my bed is a queen size – more than enough room for both of us. But we have to find your door eventually. You will still need to go into your room to get your clothes and stuff. Do you want to move your things into my room? What can we tell my mom?"

"We could tell her that we want to have a sleepover – a girl's night."

"Huh, we have a sleepover every night. She will think we are crazy if we say that. We should tell her that we're a little nervous about the ghost, that's all. I'll tell her, Holly."

"Thanks, Abby. I would feel better if I'm not alone in case the ghost comes into my room. Let's get the nails and hammer right away."

Mrs. Rizzo was busy preparing dinner when the girls once again came out to the kitchen to talk to her. She put down the knife she was using to chop vegetables and turned toward the girls. She took one look at them and knew something was up. "What's wrong girls?"

"Um Mom, we are a little nervous about sleeping alone tonight because of the ghost. Can Holly sleep in my room until Davey and Derek come back to help us find the ghost?" Abby pleaded, her green eyes darting between her mother and Holly.

"Honey, what's going on? Why are you so nervous? Did you see the ghost?"

"No Mom, but I think the ghost is playing games with us by taking our stuff and hiding it somewhere." Abby was careful not to say anything about the secret passageways. She didn't want to share their find with her mother until she had time to explore them more. Abby had a strange feeling that there was something hidden in them and she wanted to find whatever it was before anyone else.

"Oh honey, I thought we discussed that already. You will probably find the stuff soon."

"Well, I guess, but Holly is nervous too and doesn't want to sleep in her room."

Holly stepped forward. "Aunt Jane, I really am nervous. Would it be okay if I slept in Abby's room for a little while?"

"Okay dear. I'm sorry you are frightened. Of course you can stay in Abby's room. It will be fun like a girls' sleepover."

Abby looked at Holly and both girls chuckled surprising Mrs. Rizzo.

"What's so funny, girls?"

"Oh nothing, Mom! Thanks, it will be fun being in the same room."

"Please don't stay up too late talking. You should get your sleep so you can get up early for school."

"Sure Mom, no problem," Abby happily consented.

"Thank you, Aunt Jane," Holly voiced her relief.

"You're welcome, Holly. Girls, please set the table for me. Your father is coming home tonight and I made his favorite, roast beef and roasted potatoes."

"Mm, my favorite too, Mom!" Abby said as her mouth watered.

"It will be good to see Dad. He has been gone for a week."

"Yes, I know, dear. I miss him too. Besides once he is home he has a lot of things to catch up on in this house. I have a 'honey do list' for him. I don't know how happy he'll be to be home once he sees it," Mrs. Rizzo chuckled.

"Does he know about the ghost, Aunt Jane?" Holly queried.

"I haven't discussed it with him. I don't think he has seen it either. Do you girls want to tell him or should I?"

"Um, maybe we should, Mom," Abby said without hesitation.

"Well, give him some time to get settled and tell him after dinner, okay honey?"

"Sure Mom, no problem."

"Hi honey, I'm home!" was heard by all and they ran out to the hall to greet the long lost father/uncle/husband.

"Hi Dad! Great to have you home!"

"Thanks, Abby. It's good to be home."

"How are you all doing?"

"We're doing fine, dear. How was your trip?"

"Hi, Uncle Bob." Holly leaned in with a kiss and hug after Abby and her aunt finished their greetings.

"Tiring but good. I made the sale and my boss is happy. I don't have any more trips for at least two months, thank goodness. I know I need to do some things around the house for you, honey. I promise to get to them soon."

Mrs. Rizzo smiled and nodded to the girls as they all chuckled.

"Yes, I'm afraid you do, dear. I know you will do your best to make a dent in it. Let's not worry about it tonight. You need to take it easy and unwind."

"Thanks, Jane. I figured as much, honey," Bob laughed in response and continued, "I will get to it soon."

"As soon as you clean up, we can eat. Okay, Bob?"

"Ah, I'm starved and it smells so good! Did you make what I think you did, Jane?"

"Oh, come out to the kitchen and find out after you freshen up." Jane smiled with a wink.

The girls were tense and couldn't wait to finish up their dinner so they could tell Abby's father about the ghost. They couldn't help themselves and had second helpings. It was so delicious.

They waited for their mother to nod her assent so that they could begin their explanation. Abby planned to fill her father in right after he ate his dessert, a thick slice of apple pie.

Coffee was brought out with the pie and everyone stopped talking to enjoy it. Once the last fork was dropped onto the plates Abby looked over at her mother.

"Okay, Abby, why don't you, Holly, and your father go sit in the living room and catch up. Bob, we will talk more about this later. The girls want to tell you first about this."

"Jane, what's **this** all about?"

"Don't worry, Bob. Everything is all right. Let the girls tell you. Okay?"

"Okay, Jane, but we will talk later."

"Don't you want help cleaning up?" the girls asked as they brought their plates over to the sink.

"No, you already did half of it by bringing your plates over. Thank you. Go on."

"Thanks, Mom."

"Come on, Dad. Let's go into the living room and talk."

"Oh no, this sounds ominous. What's going on, girls?"

Once they were seated Abby began to explain about the boys coming over and what they planned to do about their ghost. She went into detail about what the ghost had done in their rooms but did not mention the secret passageway yet.

"Wow, a lot has happened in the week I left. Do you feel unsafe living here, girls?"

"Well, not really, Dad, but Holly felt uncomfortable when she found stuff moved or missing in her room. She plans to stay in my room with me for a few days. The boys will be coming over soon to check out things again."

Bob thought, *that's funny that the real estate agent didn't mention anything about ghosts. Maybe we wouldn't have bought this house. No, Jane loved it. We would have bought it anyway.*

"That's nice that you found some friends in school who are so helpful. Please be careful, okay? I don't know anything about what ghosts are capable of doing."

"No worries, Dad. We have some reading to do and the boys have been checking online for more information."

"Okay, well, if you need my help please let me know."

"We will, Dad, thanks."

"Yeah, thanks, Uncle Bob. It's good to have you home."

"Well, thank you, Holly. It's good to be home. If that is all you wanted to tell me, I will go spend some time with your mom. Good night, girls."

"Good night, Dad."

"Good night, Uncle Bob."

The girls waited to be alone to discuss the case further.

"Let's go look for a book to read. Maybe we can find something about this house on the shelves."

"Okay, you go to the left and I will check on the right, Abby."

"Let's worry about nailing the door tomorrow, Holly. With Dad home I feel a lot safer. Maybe the ghost won't bother us with him around."

"Okay, Abby, if you say so." Holly kept a watch for any signs of movement from the doorway behind the shelf.

The hunt was on for the girls but unbeknownst to them the ghost was already leaving something in their rooms for their bedtime reading.

CHAPTER TEN

Doing Research

Aunt Gigi sat at her crystal ball and spoke with Mianna. Well, not really spoke but used her mind to speak with the spirit of her deceased cat. She used her powers across time and space to commune with Mianna to find out about the ghosts at Sheridan House.

Mianna shared with Aunt Gigi some surprising things about the house and its many ghosts over the years. Aunt Gigi made note of these ghosts and planned to discuss her findings with the twins on their next visit.

***

Davey and Derek were busy doing their own research on their father's computer about the Sheridan House. What they found was intriguing to say the least.

Evidently there were other inhabitants of the house before the Sheridan's. They were a young couple with three children, two girls, Endora and Elena, seven and five, and a boy, Ethan, nine. The Enders family, didn't live there long when they abruptly moved after Elena had a tragic accident. She fell down the cellar stairs and died.

"Oh my God, did you see that? One of the girls fell down the cellar stairs. Isn't that what Aunt Gigi told us about Mrs. Sheridan too? But she was old. This little girl was only five. That would have been an awful thing for the family to deal with. No wonder they moved so suddenly," Davey sighed deeply affected.

"Oh, that is sad. She was only a baby." Derek hid his face as he quickly wiped away a tear before his brother noticed.

"We should share this information with Aunt Gigi and the girls. I bet they don't know about this," Davey exclaimed clearly excited to have something to tell them.

"When are we going back to the girls' house, Davey? Didn't Mrs. Rizzo say she was going to call Mom and invite our family to dinner?"

"Yeah, but I don't know when that was going to be."

"We should prepare Mom for that call. Do you think she will want to go over there? What about Dad?"

"Derek, what's with all the questions? Why don't we go ask Mom? If she says 'yes,' Dad will go along with her."

"He he, does he have a choice, Davey?"

"No, he doesn't," Davey chuckled in reply.

As the boys headed down to the kitchen where their mother was preparing dinner, the phone rang. They raced to pick it up but didn't make it in time before their mother grabbed it.

"Hello, yes, this is Laura Donato. Oh, hi, Jane. How are you?"

The boys' listened intently to the one-sided conversation trying to decipher what was being said on the other end. All the time they were doing this they watched their mother's reaction as she spoke.

"Okay, thank you very much, Jane. Yes, that's good for us. We look forward to it. I'll bring dessert. Okay, thanks, see you Saturday. Goodbye."

The boys' eyes were glued to their mother as they waited for her to announce the dinner invitation.

"Well, you probably know what that was about, huh boys? Were you going to tell me about this or did you forget?"

"Um, we were coming down to tell you, Mom. Are we going over for dinner?"

"Yes, Davey. Mrs. Rizzo was kind enough to invite all of us. I couldn't say 'no' to her. It will be nice to meet our new neighbors though anyway. So don't worry, boys, you're not in trouble."

The twins sighed in relief as they shared "TT" and smiled.

Wow, that was a close one, Davey!

Yeah, I'm relieved that Mom was okay with it.

Should we share what we found with her about the ghosts yet?

Maybe later after we talk to Aunt Gigi and the girls. I want to go to the house first and see what we find there.

"Boys, get cleaned up for dinner and tell your father to come out. We're about ready." Aggy raced around the kitchen after the boys more than ready to eat.

"Okay, Mom. Oh, when are we going to the Rizzo's house for dinner?"

"On Saturday, Davey. Mrs. Rizzo said you could bring your friend, Mickey, too, if you want. She seems to be quite taken with him by the sound of her invitation."

"Yeah, that is funny! You know Mickey. He has a way with women," Derek chuckled, amused with the idea of Mickey and his charms.

"Should I call him, Davey?"

"Sure, why not? He said he wanted to go back again."

"Okay, let me call him after we eat. He's probably having dinner now too."

"Okay boys, let's eat. When you call Mickey, tell him we will pick him up at 5:50. Mrs. Rizzo said to come at 6:00."

Shortly afterwards, the boys called Mickey and were surprised to hear that he was happy to go. He sounded excited to go for dinner and ghost hunting afterwards.

They filled him in on what they had found about the previous owners of the Sheridan House and the sad circumstances of two accidents with the cellar stairs. The boys talked a little more, and Derek closed off by saying, "Look forward to seeing you, Cat. We haven't told the girls yet about this stuff but we can fill them in after dinner on Saturday. See ya later."

"Wow, Mickey was really excited about going over to the Rizzo's house. We should start calling it the Rizzo House, shouldn't we? The Sheridan's have been gone for a long time."

"Yeah, you're right, Derek. It is kind of creepy to say it belongs to some people who have been dead for fifty or so years."

"Well, their ghosts may still be haunting the house though. Maybe they think they still own it. They definitely don't want to leave it. That is, if they are the ghosts and not the other owners."

"Do you mean to say the little girl may be a ghost too?"

"There's definitely more than one ghost, Derek. Anything is possible."

"Ooh, I hope not, Davey. It's really too creepy to think about."

"I agree, Derek, but we must be ready for anything. We should call Aunt Gigi before we go over to the Rizzo's. We better pick up the ghost flasher thing. We'll be going over there tomorrow after school. We can pick it up at that time and fill Aunt Gigi in on everything else too."

"Okay, that'll work. I keep forgetting it's only Thursday. I wish it were Saturday already. Can't wait to get over there and catch us a ghost!" Derek chuckled.

CHAPTER ELEVEN

Ghostly Gifts

The girls organized their stuff for the morning. Holly went back and forth from her room to Abby's carrying her book bag and all her clothes for a couple of days. She passed by her bed on the last run through and noticed an opened book lying on the end table. Holly picked it up leaving it opened and ran back to Abby's room with all her stuff in tow.

"What's the hurry, Holly? Did you see a ghost?" Abby couldn't help but laugh.

"No silly, I didn't, but look what I did find."

"What is it?"

"It appears that our ghost left me a gift. It's a book about this house. It was written by someone who stayed here when it was a bed and breakfast."

"Let me see that, Holly. Oh, look at this! It says that this man found some of his belongings were taken by a ghost. He says he actually saw the ghost taking some of his stuff."

"What did the ghost look like? Does he say? Was it a man or a woman?"

"He says here that it was a young woman."

"Let's read some more. It looks like our ghost wants us to know about her."

The girls got ready for bed and snuggled up under the covers with the book. After an hour of reading the girls yawned and put the book aside preparing to go to sleep but that was not to be.

Floating around Abby's desk was a long flowing white figure. It floated closer to the girls and they held their breaths unable to scream until it dropped a book on the bed and disappeared through the secret door. The girls screamed and screamed until Abby's mother and father came running into the room.

"What's wrong girls? Are you all right?"

"We saw…we saw..."

"Jane get the girls a cup of hot cocoa. I think they have had a fright."

"Yes, dear, I think you're right." Jane left the room to get the cocoa.

"Girls, you are safe. There's nothing here. What did you see?" Abby's father asked in a soft, calm voice.

Abby answered clearly still shaken by the ghostly presence, "We...we saw a ghost, Dad! It was a ghost! It was a woman and she dropped a book on my bed. I couldn't scream at first until she disappeared. I can't believe it! We saw a ghost!"

"Okay, sweetheart. You're okay. It probably won't come back. I think you frightened it too." Mr. Rizzo tried to calm his daughter as he felt his own heart pounding in disbelief.

"Is this what you saw too, Holly?"

"Yes...I can't believe it! There was a ghost...a ghost came here from the door in the wall. I can't stay here!"

"Okay, Holly. Let's calm down. I will check the house and make sure everything is locked. Where did the ghost come from? You said in the wall?"

Abby grabbed onto Holly's hand and squeezed it in warning about giving away their secret door.

"Oh, I don't know, Uncle Bob. It was there standing at the desk and floated over to us. It didn't have a face only long hair, and a flowing white gown, and it came toward us. I was so frightened I couldn't breathe."

"Let me see the book it gave you."

The girls were still in shock and had forgotten about the book that the ghost had dropped on the bed.

Abby picked it up and turned it over and gasped. It was a diary. The name on the book was Endora Enders. Who was Endora Enders?

Abby handed it to her father. He took it and opened it but closed it quickly and handed it back to the girls, trying to keep his hands from shaking. He didn't want the girls to see how anxious he, too, felt.

"I think the ghost wanted you girls to read this, not me. It seems she has something to tell you."

Jane walked in with a tray of hot cocoa and cookies for the girls. "Here girls, have some cocoa and a cookie and you will feel better. I bet the ghost won't bother you any more tonight. It didn't threaten you in any way, did it?"

"No, it was a woman, Mom. It left this book for us to read. It also left a book in Holly's room for her to read. It was about this house when it was a bed and breakfast. The man who wrote it said he saw a woman ghost too."

"Well, that's interesting. So, this ghost has been around for a long time. She desires to leave and requires your help. These books that she left are clues for you to solve the mystery of why the ghost is trapped here. You should share this with the boys too. Maybe they can help solve this mystery and help release the ghost." Jane looked over at her husband who was as dazed as she and the girls now felt. She tried to speak slowly and carefully as she observed the girls as they drank their hot cocoa. Hot cocoa always helped in times like this. But who had times like this?! She took the empty cups and the tray from the girls while trying to keep her unsteady hands still.

"Are you okay now, girls?" Bob asked not wanting to leave the girls alone yet.

"We're okay now, Dad. I think the ghost wants us to read these books. I don't think she will come back tonight, at least I hope not!"

"I think you're right, Abby, dear. You are together and there is safety in numbers. We are right across the hall if you feel uncomfortable. You can always get your sleeping bags and pillows and camp out in our room tonight, if you want."

"Umm, I guess we're okay, huh, Holly?"

"Yeah, I think we're okay, Aunt Jane. Thank you. Maybe we'll read a little of this diary before we go to sleep."

"Okay, but try to relax. The cocoa will help you sleep. You are safe, girls. We're close. Okay? Feel free to come to our room if you want to." Jane bent and kissed her daughter and niece on their cheeks, tucked them in and walked out of the room with the tray.

"Good night, girls. Sleep well. Don't worry. Call me if you need me. Okay?" Bob smiled and threw kisses their way.

***

Bob and Jane settled down in their bed with books in their hands that they couldn't read with their minds in turmoil.

"I can't believe this, Robert! The girls actually saw a ghost. What should we do? Do you think they are in danger from this ghost? Do you think that we should get a ghost expert to come in and try to exorcise it?"

"I don't think we have to worry yet. It seems the ghost is trying to give the girls clues about herself. Let's sleep on it. The girls appear to be okay but it was quite a fright for them. Has this ghost only appeared to them so far?"

"Yes, but I did feel a cold spot outside the den last week but never a ghost appearance."

"Oh, honey, I forgot to tell you, the Donato's are coming over for dinner on Saturday. The girls told you about the twin boys, Davey and Derek, who are junior detectives. They asked the boys to come help exorcise the ghost."

"So, you say these twins are junior detectives? They most likely have wonderful imaginations. Ha!"

"Don't judge them too harshly. They are great kids, so well-mannered. They have had four other cases that they've solved, Abby told me. Surprising, huh?"

"Yes, to say the least. Good for them. Well, I look forward to meeting them and their parents."

"Should I go peek in on the girls again, honey?"

"I'll do that. I'd sleep more peacefully if I knew that they were more relaxed."

Jane tiptoed across the hall and stuck her head into Abby's room. The girls were still awake with their heads together in the books. She cleared her throat to get their attention.

"Hi girls. How are you doing?"

"Hi Mom, we're fine now. We've been reading about the ghost. We'll have a lot to share with Davey and Derek when they come over on Saturday, right? We may figure this out with their help."

"Yes, on Saturday. That's nice, girls. It's time you get some sleep. You have school tomorrow. You can do some more reading tomorrow night."

"Can we read a little more to finish up the last pages of this section, Mom?"

"All right, but after that, go to sleep."

"Okay, Mom. Thanks."

"Sleep well, girls. See you in the morning."

***

The girls read a little more from each book. Holly scanned over the book that the ghost had left her about the former bed and breakfast. The man who wrote the book mentioned that he had found out the ghost was the daughter of the owner at that time. She was only nineteen years old when she had died. It was reported that the girl had died from a broken heart. The man she loved had left her for another woman and had the audacity to return to the bed and breakfast with his pregnant wife. The young girl, Felicity, was shocked and never got over the fact that the man she loved, who said he loved her too, had discarded her.

Holly shared this with Abby. "Can you believe a man would do that to someone he professed to love? No wonder she died of a broken heart."

"How can someone die of a broken heart, Holly? Maybe she refused to eat and died of lack of nourishment most likely."

"Maybe, but if you lost the one person you loved most in this world, I think it would break your heart."

"Well, maybe. I hope I never find out."

"Yeah, me too. We must help Felicity leave here. She has to go to the other side and finally be at peace along with all the other ghosts she may be holding back in this house."

"You're right, Holly. We should tell the boys tomorrow at lunch about these books and our ghostly visit. They will go out of their minds!" Abby chuckled but got goosebumps all over thinking about the ghost.

The girls closed the books but not before looking around the room especially over at the hidden door in the wall before shutting off the nightstand light and making sure the night light was on.

"Are you okay, Holly?"

"Yeah, sure. That's why I am here with you. I don't think nails would have kept the ghost out of the room, Abby? Did you see how she flew right through the wall?"

"I did, Holly. You're right! Well, we'll have got to find a way to help this ghost find her way to the other side soon. I don't think I could take another scare like she gave us tonight."

"I agree, Abby. I'm still trembling. Well, let's try to relax and get to sleep. Six-thirty comes too early."

"Right! Good night Holly."

"Good night, Abby."

Abby whispered into her pillow, "Good night, Felicity, or whoever you are."

CHAPTER TWELVE

Revelations Revealed

The boys had no idea that they would be blown away by all the disclosures that the girls would reveal to them. Their day was following the usual boring, slow as molasses pace until lunch.

Abby and Holly hurried through the lunch line grabbing their choices and heading over to their table. They kept their eyes open for the boys and noticed them standing in the lunch line.

Abby waved at Davey and motioned for him to come over and sit with them. Davey waved and nodded back.

As the boys got closer to the table they could not only see but feel the charge going on between Abby and Holly. The girls' eyes were wide and they were nervously tapping their feet under the table.

The twins used "TT" to discuss this.

Wow, look at the girls, Davey! They are nearly jumping out of their seats. Something could have happened at the house.

Yeah, I can see the anxiety in their faces and their posture.

Shh, let's find out what they have to say. It must be a doozy!

"Hi boys," the girls announced together much to the boys' surprise.

"Hi girls," Davey and Derek mimicked back.

"Abby, you start first, okay," Holly said anxiety evident in her wobbly voice.

Davey couldn't stay still and asked, "What's wrong, Abby? Did something happen last night?"

"Oh boy, did something happen last night! You won't believe what we found out or what we saw!"

"Okay, tell me please! You are making me nervous!"

"Sorry Davey, but we need to keep our voices down we don't want anyone else to hear this."

Abby whispered in Davey's ear about their ghostly visit and gifts and who the ghost could be.

Davey's eyes got wider and wider as he listened intently. He was simultaneously using "TT" to inform Derek what Abby was saying.

Holly leaned into Derek and began to tell him about the book the ghost had given her. His eyes were wide and alert, too, over all these incredible findings. He was loving every minute of this.

The kids all sat back and sighed after the surprises were uncovered. The boys were still awestruck over everything the girls shared.

"I can't believe this, Abby! Now we have a better idea of at least who three of the ghosts are. The woman you saw was most likely Felicity and through her sadness she had kept the ghosts of the little girl, Elena, and Mrs. Sheridan locked up here with her."

"Remember I said I saw a little wispy thing floating around in the corridor? I bet that was the little girl and the cold spot was probably Mrs. Sheridan. The little girl could be the mischievous one who is taking and moving your things around."

"Wow, that sounds possible, Davey," Abby whispered excitedly.

"I remember reading about ghosts and how their age at death affects how strong their spirits are. None of them are malicious in intent so I don't see any reason to feel threatened by their appearances. The little girl probably doesn't even know that she is dead. She likes your stuff and possibly has found a place to collect it in the passageways. We can check them out tomorrow night when we come over to your house, Abby."

"Yeah, that sounds good. Our parents will be busy chatting before and after dinner and that's when we can go exploring."

Derek looked at Holly and smiled. He was feeling good to see her again but his mind was racing in all directions as he processed the information. "Holly, did you and Abby go into the passageways again?"

"Um, well, yeah we did a little. We followed the same path you did and ended up in Abby's room. I was too nervous to go any further to find the door to my room. Maybe we can do that tomorrow. I'm sleeping in Abby's room temporarily. That's where we saw the ghost but I feel safer being with her than being along."

"I understand what you mean, Holly. I would be nervous to stay in a room alone too. Davey and I sleep in separate rooms but I would probably bunk with him if that happened in our house."

Holly smiled and touched Derek on his arm and they both went back to eating their lunches.

Mrs. Trakko was moving around the room and focused on the twins. She was always trying to catch them doing something that would warrant a detention.

Davey looked up from his lunch when he spotted Mrs. Trakko and "TT" was passed between the twins.

Don't look now, Derek. Your favorite teacher is heading this way. She looks like she is looking for a reason to put us in detention.

Really, Derek, don't look!

Oops, sorry, Bro. I couldn't help it. I gave her one of my charming smiles that I borrowed from Cat. It always works for him.

Ha, funny! Let's eat and get a move on. We don't want her to find a reason to detain us.

No problem, food's already gone. Ha!

The girls observed the twins as they gobbled down the rest of their lunches and excused themselves saying, "Sorry to rush out, Abby and Holly, but Mrs. Trakko is heading this way. See you tomorrow at 6:00. Can't wait to meet your ghosts."

"Okay, Davey. See you later," Abby replied with disappointment in her voice

Holly waved and smiled at Derek.

He gave Holly a goofy smile and backed away passing by Mrs. Trakko who gave him a steely gaze that threatened to penetrate his skull.

"Phew, that was a close call. I swear that woman is out to get us, or maybe you, Derek! Ha!"

"No, I think she even has it in for you too, Davey."

"Do you believe all that has transpired since we were at Abby's house last? Wait until we fill Cat in. He won't believe it! He will actually be speechless for once."

"Now that would be funny!" Derek chuckled.

***

The girls finished up shortly after the boys and headed to their last classes of the day.

"They were certainly in a hurry all of a sudden, huh, Abby?"

"Yeah, Davey said it was Mrs. Trakko. I guess they haven't been on good terms in her class."

"She's a tough one, Abby. I don't particularly enjoy being in her class either. I am so quiet I disappear there. That way she can't find any reason to give me detention."

"I don't think you have any worries about that, Holly. Mrs. Trakko likes you. She always calls on the students that she doesn't like. If you raise your hand a lot she smiles at you and moves onto someone who doesn't have a hand up."

"Yes, I noticed that too. She likes to catch those who didn't study or that fall asleep in her class. I don't think the twins would do that. They are both highly intelligent."

"Well, yes, they are, Holly. But if you notice they do tend to zone out a lot. Maybe it has something to do with being twins. They think inside each other's heads."

"Do you think so, Abby? I suppose that could be it. They think like one person."

"Yeah, but they sure are cute as two separate people. I think they like us too, Holly. It will certainly be interesting tomorrow night. I wonder if the ghost will make an appearance for them. She may be a little timid with boys. After all she was hurt by a man and may dislike all males for that reason."

"Do you think we will be able to talk to her?"

"I guess we could try to correspond in some way."

"I can't wait for the boys to come over. I really enjoy them. They will be a great help to us. We should let them read a little of the books too before we begin our hunt."

"Yeah, sure, that would work. They are thorough and will want to see the books," Holly agreed, and continued, "They may have some answers for us about helping release the ghosts."

"I certainly hope so, Holly," Abby responded with a sigh.

CHAPTER THIRTEEN

A Ghost Flasher Lesson

Davey and Derek rushed home to let Aggy out and ran around the yard with her. They wanted to give her some much-needed attention. There never seemed to be enough time to play with her. They were always working on the case. They promised to make it up to her over the weekend. They gave Aggy a couple of treats, filled her water bowl, locked up, and jumped on their bikes.

They couldn't wait to tell Aunt Gigi all that had transpired in a short time. She would certainly have something to add to all this.

Davey, we can't forget to ask Aunt Gigi for the ghost flasher.

I won't forget. I promise. This is too important to forget, Derek. Aunt Gigi is going to be surprised that so much has happened since we last saw her.

Do you think she may somehow know? Nothing she does or says will surprise me.

Me neither, Bro! Ha!

Remember to keep our minds open to Aunt Gigi while we are at Abby's. That way she can commune with us and Mianna at the same time. We may need all the help we can get too, Davey.

Yup, I agree. Let's get moving faster. Are you an old man or what?

Hey, wait up, Davey! You did do something to your bike! I knew it! Wait for meeee!

Davey pulled out ahead and was waiting at the top of Aunt Gigi's stairs as Derek parked his bike next to Davey's and walked up the stairs clearly disgruntled.

Aunt Gigi was watching the boys and opened the door with her arms extended. The boys ignored her arms and deftly walked around them much to the amusement of their aunt.

"Well, boys. How are you doing today? How's my Aggy girl doing?"

"Hi Aunt Gigi. We're fine and so is Aggy," Davey chirped in a better mood than his brother.

"Hey Derek, what's up with you? You don't look too happy?"

"Aww, Davey beat me again. He keeps revving up his bike. It's not fair!" Derek harrumphed.

"Oh, I see. Maybe you can work together on yours to make it compatible to Davey's. Isn't that possible, Davey?" Aunt Gigi smiled sweetly at the boys waiting for a response.

"Um, oh sure, Aunt Gigi. We'll do it soon."

"Okay, Derek? All better now? I hate to see you two angry with one another. It upsets me and also your abilities to be receptive to one another and to me and Mianna. Let's clear our minds, boys."

"Okay, did you hear that Derek? Your mood will affect how we handle our case. Snap out of it, Bro!"

"Yeah, you too Davey. I'm fine since you promised to fix my bike to be like yours."

Stop worrying about it, Derek. We should tell Aunt Gigi what happened at Abby's yesterday.

Okay, sorry.

"Aunt Gigi, there's a ton of stuff to tell you about Abby's ghosts. You won't believe what the girls found out," Davey exclaimed with flushed cheeks and an animated expression on his face.

The boys took turns filling in their aunt about the ghost's appearance and her gifts of two books.

Aunt Gigi listened intently not interrupting until the boys sat back on the couch and smiled happily.

"Wow, you did have a lot to tell me. It's all enlightening to say the least. It's evident that the ghost, the main one, is a young lady, Felicity. She suffered a great loss and received a shock when her boyfriend returned with his pregnant wife. She never got over this shock. It sounds like she pined away and stopped eating and died of malnutrition."

"Yes, that's what we thought too, Aunt Gigi. No one can die from a broken heart, can they?" Davey asked.

"Well, it is not unheard of. But, let's not get into that. What you must do, boys, is to read all you can from the book and diary that the girls were given. The ghost is actively seeking help by her recent appearance and actions. You go to the last place she was spotted and sit and wait for her to come to you while actively speaking out to her in calm voices. Tell her that you understand what she went through and want to help her leave her prison in the house. Explain to her that she has to go to the other side where she will find peace and her family waiting for her."

"Okay, we can do that with the girls' help. The ghost appeared to the girls and evidently feels comfortable sharing with them."

"All you are required to do is appear non-threatening to Felicity. She doesn't particularly like men. But you and Derek are not men. Please don't come on too strong with her, okay?"

"Okay, Aunt Gigi. I think we can do that. Right Derek?"

"Sure. Oh, Aunt Gigi, we need to use the ghost flasher for tomorrow night. We are going over to the Rizzo's house for dinner with our family and Mickey too. Mrs. Rizzo took a shine to Mickey. You know how charming he can be," Derek snickered.

"Yes, I can see how that could happen. Mickey charmed me too!" Aunt Gigi giggled.

"I'll get the ghost flasher for you. Sit tight. Be right back. I have some snacks for you in the kitchen. So help yourselves."

"Ooh, snacks, let's go, Davey!"

Aunt Gigi tittered as she went to retrieve the item from the magic box in her bedroom. She quickly came back to the kitchen with the ghost flasher in her hand.

The boys were stuffing their faces neatly now because Aunt Gigi was sitting across from them. She waited until they had their fill before beginning their first lesson on catching a ghost.

"Okay boys, let's begin your first lesson on catching a ghost. Davey, do you want to try it first?"

"Um sure, Aunt Gigi," Davey said in a shaky voice.

Leaving the kitchen and going into the living room Aunt Gigi began, "Stand in front of me and put your left hand out."

Aunt Gigi placed the flasher in his left hand and instructed him, "Hold it firmly keeping your fingers free of the buttons. I told you both about these buttons and what to do but I will refresh your memories. You should point the flasher directly at the ghost. There is a red button and a yellow one. The red button is the first button you will press when you see a ghost. Once you have contained the ghost press the yellow button and it will lock the ghost or ghosts inside. The tube will glow blue once the ghost is caught. The more ghosts you have contained, the darker the shade of blue and you will hear clicks to indicate how many entities you have trapped."

"Wow that is so cool, Aunt Gigi. I can't wait to use it," Derek exclaimed excited to begin.

"Now, what I'm going to do will shock you. But listen, Boys, don't worry you are safe with me and nothing will harm you."

The twins looked at each other and gulped nervously.

What's Aunt Gigi going to do, Davey?

I don't know, but hold on tightly to your seat I feel a wild ride coming on!

Aunt Gigi pulled out her wand from inside her cloak and waved it over a figurine of a cow. The cow suddenly appeared in front of them as a ghostly image.

The boys jumped up in alarm but calmed down again once Aunt Gigi waved her hand over them.

"Davey, please point the flasher directly at the ghost cow and press the red button firmly."

Davey listened attentively and did as he was told. Much to his surprise and delight the ghost cow disappeared.

"Davey, quickly press the yellow button."

Davey pressed the yellow button and watched the tube as it turned sky blue.

Davey couldn't contain his excitement and jumped up and down. "Derek, did you see that? I did it! I contained the ghost!"

"Wow, I saw that, Davey! Can I try it Aunt Gigi?"

"Sure, wait a minute. Let me free the cow and put her back on the shelf where she belongs. Okay, Derek, your turn."

Derek stepped up to replace Davey and took the flasher out of his hand. Davey, however, was a little reluctant to release it.

"Thank you, Bro. I want to try it too."

"Sorry, Derek. It was too cool. Wait until you do it. The tube becomes a little heavier and warmer."

"Yes, you will feel something there. The more ghosts you have contained the heavier, warmer and bluer the tube will become. You need to hold onto it firmly and don't let go, even if it feels like it is pulling out of your hand. Once you leave the building you do the reserve, press the yellow button, and next, the red one to release the ghosts. They will dissipate into the air and be free to go to the other side and never return."

Aunt Gigi repeated the same instructions for Derek with the same results.

Derek, too, was excited and smiled broadly as he chuckled in delight. "Wow, that was way cool, Davey! I see what you mean. It felt a little heavier but not much. I imagine with more ghosts it will feel heavier and hotter to touch. We will need to be careful with this. We might have got to hold onto it together to bring it outside Abby's house to release the ghosts once and for all."

"I think you have it down pat, boys. If for some reason you cannot contain the ghosts, you should open your mind to me immediately and say my name. I will tell you in your minds what to do next. I'm sure you will not have any problems but remember I am close by in your mind if you want help."

"Thank you, Aunt Gigi. We appreciate that, right Davey?"

"Most definitely, Aunt Gigi. Thank you!"

"What time are you going to the Rizzo's house tomorrow night?"

"Mom said they expect us at 6:00."

"Okay, I will be thinking of you and sending good vibes your way all evening. Please be careful, boys. Ghosts can be tricky."

"We will, Aunt Gigi. Thank you," Davey and Derek answered in unison.

CHAPTER FOURTEEN

Creating Ghosts

"We have some time left before your mother gets home. Do you want to learn how to make a ghost like I did?"

"What? Wow! That would be awesome, Aunt Gigi!" Davey yelled so loud he made himself jump along with Derek.

"Yeah, that would be way cool, Aunt Gigi," Derek added for emphasis.

"Okay boys. You two are hilarious! You always give me a good laugh with your unbridled enthusiasm!" Aunt Gigi couldn't help from giggling uncontrollably while the boys looked on in mute surprise.

"Okay, are you ready?"

"Yes, yes!!" The twins chorused.

"Let's see. Which one of these animals would you like to use to create your first ghost?"

"Hmm, I think I like this giraffe, Aunt Gigi," Davey decided.

"That's a good choice, Davey."

Aunt Gigi handed the twins their wands.

"Okay, come closer to the giraffe and wave your wand over the animal. Hold the flasher in front of you pointing directly at the giraffe. Good. Yes, like that."

Davey's hands were shaking but his face was a picture of calm control.

"Davey, say these words with me and stay as still as you can, concentrating on only the giraffe. **A giraffe you are now but a ghost you will soon be on the count of 1 2 3**."

Davey pursed his lips, scrunched up his face and squinted his eyes to keep himself still and recited after Aunt Gigi.

"Nicely done so far, Davey. Okay, next step is to think of a ghostly image and project it toward the giraffe as if you were flinging something away from you without moving."

"Oops, not quite on target. You almost got me!" Aunt Gigi chuckled.

"Oh sorry, Aunt Gigi."

"That's okay, I did the same thing the first time and almost made a ghost of one of my sisters," Aunt Gigi began to laugh so hard she brought tears to her eyes.

Aunt Gigi calmed herself down and began to explain, "Try again and concentrate. Don't think of anything else but the giraffe and how it will look as a ghost."

Davey opened his mind to only the giraffe and closed his eyes and concentrated harder than he ever had. When he opened his eyes again the little giraffe was now a wispy ghost in front of him.

"Oh wow, I did it, Aunt Gigi! I did it, Derek! Do you see it? I made a ghost!" Davey chortled with a wide smile that lit up the room.

"Very impressive for the first time, my boy! Congratulations! Point the flasher directly at the ghost giraffe and press the red button followed by the yellow one."

Davey followed directions and beamed as the tube turned light blue. He held it up for Derek to see and admire his work.

"Wow, Davey, that's great! You did it! Can I try it, Aunt Gigi, please?"

"Of course, dear boy, but let Davey put the giraffe back on the shelf. We don't want the poor thing stuck in the flasher for all eternity."

"Davey, point the flasher toward the shelf and imagine, in your mind, what it looked like before you turned it into a ghost; and press the buttons one at a time. Get closer to the shelf. There it is, back to its rightful spot. Wonderful job, Davey!"

Turning toward Derek who couldn't keep still, Aunt Gigi instructed, "Derek, first of all, control your movements. You should stand as still as you can for this to work like Davey did. I know you can do it. Take your wand and the flasher in your hands and pick out which animal you want to make into a ghost."

Derek looked up and down the shelves until he came to a lion. It would be super cool to make one into a ghost, he thought.

"Ah, I see you picked my lion friend. Nice choice, Derek. Okay, like I told Davey, you calm yourself down and stand very still, wave your wand over the animal while thinking only of the lion and imagining him as a ghost and repeat after me. **A lion you are now but a ghost you will soon be on the count of 1 2 3**."

Derek squinted his eyes and furrowed his brow in deep concentration as he looked at the lion, waved his wand, and repeated what Aunt Gigi said. In seconds the lion appeared in front of Derek as a ghost.

"Oh, my God! I can't believe I did it! Davey, look at this lion ghost!! Incredible, huh?"

"Wow, that is cool, Derek! Look the lion is roaring but we can't hear him! That is too funny!"

"Yes, he is, boys, and I don't think he is too happy to be a ghost. Push the buttons quickly, Derek. Let's get him back on the shelf before he does something."

"Huh, does something, Aunt Gigi? What can he do? He is only a ghost that we created. He can't possibly do anything to us, can he?"

Derek's hands shook as he tried to control the flasher that had captured the ghost lion. The lion appeared to be trying to get out of the flasher."

Aunt Gigi ignored his question and continued, "Okay, Derek, do you know what to do next?"

"Um, yes, I think so." Derek pressed the correct buttons and concentrated as the ghost lion appeared back on the shelf as a figurine once again much to his relief.

"No worries, boys. But, remember **never** to use this power on anyone or anything without me being there. Strange things could happen." Aunt Gigi raised her eyebrows in warning.

"Oh, okay, Aunt Gigi. We promise we won't. But what if it happens by accident if we concentrate too hard on something?"

"Well, the thing you make into a ghost could stay a ghost unless you capture it in the flasher and return it to its original state."

"We would need the flasher to do that."

"Yes, you would. So please be careful. I only have one of these flashers. Guard it with your life." Aunt Gigi sent out another warning as she squinted her eyes at the boys.

"Okay, Aunt Gigi. We will guard it with our lives, won't we, Derek?"

"Oh yes, we will!" Davey looked at Derek and nodded in agreement, afraid to look at Aunt Gigi's eyes. He remembered another time when those eyes nearly fried him with their intensity. He shivered at the thought.

"Well, I guess that is the end of the lesson today, boys. You are quick learners which makes it easier for me. I have a lot to teach you yet."

"What else do you want to teach us, Aunt Gigi?" Derek ventured forth.

"Well, there is more to teach you with your wands, hats and capes."

"We don't have hats and capes, Aunt Gigi," Davey announced in surprise.

"Oh, that's right. I haven't given you the hats and capes yet. Ah yes, on your next birthday I will give you both one of them. At that time, we will begin another lesson using the items."

"Oh, which one are you going to give us, Aunt Gigi?" Derek's eyes widened in anticipation.

"I can't tell you that. It wouldn't be a surprise now would it? I really shouldn't have told you anything. Sorry about that. I guess I am forgetful sometimes. I need to work on that," Aunt Gigi chuckled making deep dimples appear on her cheeks.

"Okay, I like to be surprised anyway, Aunt Gigi. Don't you, Derek?"

"Yeah, I guess so. But whichever you give us will be awesome, Aunt Gigi. I can't wait until our birthday."

"Well you do have nearly ten months to go yet." Aunt Gigi's face crinkled in a warm smile that lit up her eyes.

"Oh well, I guess we can wait. But in the meantime, you can teach us other stuff, right?"

"Sure, Davey, there is a lot more I could teach you. Boys, please help me clean up the kitchen and put away the snacks. It's almost time for you to head home. Don't forget, Davey, to help your brother with his bike. Okay? I hate to see him unhappy."

"Oh, I won't forget, Aunt Gigi. I always keep my promises to him."

"Good to know, Davey. You are good boys. I'm proud of you and how much you have learned and accomplished. Good luck tomorrow at the Rizzo's house and remember keep your minds open to me. I will be there to help you that way if you have any difficulty. Oh, don't forget the ghost flasher, boys. You are going to want that." Aunt Gigi handed it to Davey and patted him on the arm sending strength and good luck his way.

"Oh, I can't believe we almost forgot it again, Derek! Thank you, Aunt Gigi. We'll let you know how things go and keep our minds open to you and Mianna."

"Good. Mianna will be happy to hear that."

"Thank you for everything today, Aunt Gigi," Davey said and out of the blue added, "We love you!"

"Oh my goodness! Thank you, boys!! You made my day! I love you too!"

Aunt Gigi stood at the door and watched the boys ride away. She wore a bigger smile than usual that made her eyes twinkle like diamonds that shot out sparks. If only the boys could have seen her.

Further down the road the twins used "TT".

Wow, I can't believe you said that, Davey?

Why? I do love Aunt Gigi, don't you?

Of course, but we don't announce it like that. We don't say that stuff much.

Well, maybe we should more often. Aunt Gigi is a wonderful aunt. She's like no other. No one has a witch for an aunt, and may I add, a good witch for that matter. That's important.

Yeah, I guess you're right, Davey. Sorry. It's hard for me to say sometimes. I know Mom wants to hear it so I say it to her only.

Well, I love you, Derek.

Ugh! Davey!

Davey pulled away from Derek leaving him in his dust once again. He didn't want his brother to see the wide grin on his face.

"I'll get you, Davey!" Derek yelled but not in an angry way. He felt amused and pretty good. He loved Davey back but didn't want to tell him. Maybe one day, he thought.

CHAPTER FIFTEEN

Time with Aggy

Aggy was having a wonderful time playing outside with the boys. She chased her ball when the boys threw it and grabbed a stick and teased them with it. She loved playing tug of war with her favorite rope toy. She kept the twins busy all morning until lunch. It appeared that she was trying to catch up from the whole week being stuck in the house.

Davey and Derek sat down on the steps to rest and watch Aggy chase her ball for the umpteenth time.

"Where does Aggy get all this energy, Derek?"

"I think she saves it up all week for the weekend to drive us crazy and tire us out!" Davey tittered in amusement as he watched Aggy chewing on another stick.

"You may be right, Bro," Derek said as he picked up Aggy's ball that she had dropped at his feet and threw it long.

"Boys, time for lunch," Mrs. Donato called out.

"Okay, Mom, coming. Let's go, Aggy, time for lunch."

Aggy's ears perked up when she heard *lunch*. She was always ready to eat.

The boys sat and ate their peanut butter and jelly sandwiches and some potato sticks with a side of carrot sticks too. The deal was they had to eat as many carrot sticks as potato sticks or the potato sticks would be taken away.

"How many carrot sticks did you eat, Davey?"

"All of them. I like to eat the potato sticks last. That way Mom can't take them away. Ha!"

"Yes, I guess I should try that. The potato sticks taste better in the mouth last." Derek shoveled in as many carrot sticks as he could to get them out of the way first."

"Derek, be careful," his mother warned as she watched him stuff another carrot stick into his already full mouth.

Derek nodded to his mother since he was unable to say a word.

"I don't know about you sometimes!" His mother voiced her exasperation but smiled in amusement.

"After you finish up your lunch, clean your rooms and bring down all your dirty clothes. I am washing today."

"Okay, Mom. We will," Davey answered now that he had finished up his potato sticks before Derek.

"Please put your dishes in the dishwasher too."

"Yes Mom," Derek responded after finishing his potato sticks.

After lunch the boys headed upstairs chatting by "TT" with Aggy in tow after she had eaten her share of doggy snacks.

Should we be preparing for tonight, Davey?

What should we do to prepare, Derek?

Oh, I don't know. We can practice with the ghost flasher.

Oh, no you don't. You are not going to get me into trouble with Aunt Gigi. Did you forget her eyes?

Ha, no I didn't, Bro. But we should be practicing what we are going to do when we see the ghosts.

I'm not worried, Derek. We will know what to do. We practiced with Aunt Gigi and as long as we keep our minds open to her and Mianna we will be fine.

Okay, if you say so. Let's look at our list of stuff that we know so far about the ghosts. Afterwards, we can ask questions of anything that is missing. Okay?

Sure, Derek.

So far the marker board listed the following:

1. Three ghosts in the Rizzo's house
2. Main ghost? Felicity
3. Second ghost – Elena, little girl
4. Third ghost – Mrs. Sheridan
5. Felicity seen by Abby & Holly
6. Cold spots - ? Mrs. Sheridan
7. Cold spots felt by Cat, girls & Mrs. Rizzo
8. Wisp of a ghost - ? Elena

9. Wisp seen by Davey, Me and Abby
10. Ghost - ? Felicity seen by Abby and Holly - gave girls two books

"Wow, we have a lot of information here, Davey. Anything you want to add?"

"No, not until after we go to the Rizzo's. We may have much more to add then. In fact we may even have captured the ghosts."

"Do you think we will be that lucky the first time using the ghost flasher, Davey?"

"Um, maybe. After all it won't be the first time we have used it. Remember we both used it to capture our own animal ghosts. Ha! That was so cool!"

"Yeah, it was, Bro. I wish we could practice again though."

"Enough about that, Derek. I feel like a broken record and playing the same song again and again for you. The answer is *no*!"

"Yeah, I guess you're right. Sorry, Davey."

"I can't believe you Derek. Remember the eyes! Aunt Gigi burned the image inside my head!"

"Ha ha, yeah, I know, I know, Davey, you can't forget that. You came so close to being incinerated!"

"I don't think that's at all funny, Derek! If she directed those eyes on you, you would know what I mean."

"Okay, I give. Sorry." Derek moved away from his brother so Davey wouldn't see the smirk and amusement in his eyes.

"We better clean up our rooms like Mom said. Go pick up all the dirty clothes in your room, Derek. I'll get mine. Hurry up."

"Okay, okay, you are sounding like Mom now, Davey! Ha-ha!"

"Well, I am the older twin after all. I can boss you around."

"Oh, no you can't."

"Yes, I can."

"Davey, cut it out!"

"Race you downstairs with my clothes."

"Ha-ha, beat you, Derek!"

"No, you didn't. I'm already down here! Ha!"

"What? How did you get down here?"

"I'll never tell." Derek smirked his way past his brother and brought his clothes to the laundry room.

"Wow! That was fast boys. Nicely done!"

"Yep, sure thing, Mom. You are welcome!" Derek laughed as he looked back at his brother who was wearing a disgruntled look.

Davey tried to keep this look on his face but didn't succeed as he and Derek broke up into laughter.

Laura shook her head as she observed her twins bent over and giggling and mumbled to herself as she piled more clothes into the washing machine.

"Mom, we're going back outside with Aggy for a while, okay?" Derek asked.

"Sure, as long as you have given me all your clothes."

"Yep, we did!" Davey yelled back as he headed for the door but stopped short as Derek asked, "What time should we be ready to go to the Rizzo's tonight?"

"I want to leave here by 5:30 or so. You both should take baths and freshen up so you are presentable."

"Oh, a bath, Mom? Really?" Derek groaned.

"Sure thing, Mom," Davey agreed and poked his brother.

Don't you want to smell good for Holly, you doofus?

Oh, yeah, forgot! Thanks, Bro.

The twins played throughout the afternoon with Aggy much to her delight. They were all exhausted after running, climbing and playing catch.

Laura looked out at them running around and smiled. What a godsend that Aggy was. She brought the whole family together and gave them so much joy. Even her husband, Dan, enjoyed playing with Aggy, and he wasn't much of a dog person.

Opening the front door Laura called out, "Okay boys, time to come in and get cleaned up."

"What time is it, Mom?" Davey looked anxious as he motioned to Derek to come with Aggy.

"It's still early, only 4:00 but I wanted to give you both enough time to get ready. Your father will be home at 5:00."

"Okay, Mom," Derek responded.

What's wrong, Davey? You look nervous.

Yeah, I guess I have butterflies in my stomach.

Why?

Oh, I don't know. I'm thinking about the ghosts and hoping they're going to be responsive to us and easy to catch.

Well, you know that Aunt Gigi will be watching. Remember to keep your mind open to her and Mianna.

Yep, I will. You too.

Sure thing.

Derek walked upstairs and didn't make eye contact with his brother for fear he would see the fear in his own eyes.

"I'll go first in the bathroom, Davey. Okay? That'll give you some time to pick out your clothes and collect your thoughts."

"Okay, sure. Thanks, Derek."

Both boys were ready by 4:45 spic and span and well-polished or so their mother told them.

"You look so handsome, boys! Wow, you really clean up well," Laura chuckled.

Dan walked in at 5:00 and looked over the troops as they stood in the kitchen all dressed up. He felt like it was Easter Sunday and said, "Well, look at all of you! Looking spic and span and well-polished."

The twins groaned and shared puzzled looks, "What does that mean anyway? What is spic and span?"

"Oh, never mind, boys. You look perfect! The girls will be pleased." Laura exchanged a smile with her husband and leaned in to give him a hug and kiss hello.

Davey and Derek made grossed out faces as they observed their parents kissing and shared "TT."

Ugh I hate to see our parents kissing, Davey!

Me too! So gross!

Who can understand them when they speak in riddles? What in the world is spic and span?

Beats me, Bro. I have no idea. Never heard of it. I guess maybe we will learn one day or not.

The boys silently chuckled in amusement.

"You have half an hour to get ready, dear. We'll be here waiting for you. We ought to pick up Mickey at quarter to six."

"Okay, honey. Be right back down in a jiffy."

"Well, what do you boys plan to do tonight after dinner? Are you going ghost hunting again?"

"Yeah, we plan to check out the place again in hopes that the specter or specters appear."

"Specter, you say? Have the girls seen a specter yet?"

Davey looked at Derek and sighed, *we better tell Mom about the sightings, huh?*

Yeah, I guess so.

"Yeah, the girls had quite an experience," Davey began.

Derek picked up from there and explained what had happened that night with the ghostly appearance and the gifts.

Davey added more information about the findings in the books and the history of the house.

"Wow that is a lot to take in. Are you nervous about seeing the ghost tonight? Please be careful. If there is a problem we are all there to help. Dad and Mr. Rizzo can chase the ghost away."

"Oh no, Mom. We don't want to chase it we want to capture it and send it to the other side."

"Oh, and how are you planning to do that?"

"Well, Aunt Gigi let us borrow her ghost flasher and taught us how to use it."

"Ghost flasher? What on earth is that?" Laura's voice relayed her anxiety even though she had confidence in her boys.

"Don't worry, Mom. We'll be fine. Aunt Gigi is keeping us in her sight by long distance, you know, with her cat, Mianna, in the crystal ball. She will make sure we are safe at all times."

"Okay, if Aunt Gigi is keeping a watch over you, I won't worry too much, only a little." Laura gave the boys a hug and kissed the top of their heads.

"Oh Mom! Don't get mushy on us, okay?" Derek squirmed trying to get away.

"I can't help it, boys. I love you and you do look pretty good in those shirts."

The boys groaned so loud that even their father heard them as he came down the stairs.

"What's going on down here? What's all the groaning for?"

"Oh, nothing Dad. We're fine."

Laura leaned into Dan and whispered, "I was giving them some love and attention. They are being boys and not too fond of the mushy displays," Laura chuckled.

Dad added a knuckle sandwich to the boys' heads that made them laugh.

"Well, it's time to go. Boys, call your friend, Mickey, to make sure he will be ready."

"Sure, Dad. Derek, you call him."

Once assured that Mickey was ready they set off for his house and to the Rizzo's for an interesting night ahead.

CHAPTER SIXTEEN

Dinner at the Rizzo's

Mickey was excited as he jumped in the back of the van with the boys. He smiled and was his usual charming self as he thanked the Donato's for picking him up.

"You're welcome, Mickey. It's always nice to see you," Mrs. Donato said as her husband grunted and nodded in agreement too busy watching the traffic ahead to acknowledge Mickey.

Turning toward the twins Mickey asked in a whisper, "What do you think we will see tonight?"

"Well, we're hoping that it will be a ghost, Cat," Derek said with amusement in his voice.

"Yeah, that's why we're here, Cat." Davey added. He too, was amused by Cat's question.

"I hope you are ready to meet the specter, Cat," Derek said as he watched Cat's face for any sign that he was going to bail out on them.

"Specter? Um yeah, I'm…I'm ready."

"Yeah, it's another word for ghost, also, phantom, spooky image, shade, wraith, and apparition. Hmm, I hope so, Cat. We may need your help keeping the girls safe while we tangle with the ghosts."

"Oh, sure. Wait a minute, did you say ghosts?"

"Yep, ghosts. Didn't you know there were more than one?"

"No, I...I...didn't know that. You didn't tell me that. I thought we were looking for one ghost."

"Don't worry, Cat. It will be fine. Davey and I will capture the phantoms."

"How...how are you going to capture them, Derek?"

"Well, our Aunt Gigi gave us a special device like we read about online. Remember there were all kinds of stuff that ghost hunters use?"

"Can I see it? Wow, where did she get it? Is she a ghost hunter?" Cat's eyes widened as he processed all this and looked at the device that Davey had pulled out of his pocket.

"No, not really. She inherited it from her relatives. At that time in history they believed in ghosts and had to exorcise them with this tool."

"Oh boy, can't wait to see you do it! When are you going to do the exorcism?" Cat was jumping up and down in the car.

"Well, someone is excited back there. What's going on, boys?" Laura asked curious to what the boys were discussing in whispers.

"Oh, nothing, Mom. We were discussing what we were going to do when we see a shade."

"A shade, you say? Really, I hope you are ready. I have never seen one myself. Let me know when you do spy it. I would like to see it too. But be careful, okay?"

"Okay, Mom, it could be dangerous."

"Really? Well, I have three brave boys to protect me, don't I?" Laura laughed and poked her husband who laughed along with her. But Laura inside was anxious about her boys doing this case. She wished she could share more with her husband but he wouldn't believe half of what she had to tell him about magic, Aunt Gigi and the boys. Maybe one day she would reveal it all to him.

The Rizzo's were at the front door as the Donato's and Mickey drove up the drive and parked.

Laura looked up at the large Victorian house and exclaimed, "Wow, this is so colorful and beautiful, honey." The Victorian stood tall and stately with its multi-colored trimmings in shades of pink, turquoise, burgundy, and cream.

"Yes, it is! Quite impressive!" Dan responded as he opened the car door for Laura.

The twins and Mickey were out first and raced up the stairs, before the adults, to be greeted by the girls.

"Hi Davey, Derek and Mickey," the girls recited happily.

"Hi. How are you Abby and Holly and oh, Mr. and Mrs. Rizzo?" Davey and Derek joined in with Cat adding his own greeting.

"It's so nice to see you boys. Happy to see you could make it, Mickey. We missed you.

"Oh, thank you, Mrs. Rizzo. I'm happy to be here. Thank you for including me."

"This is my husband, Bob Rizzo. Honey, this is the boy I told you about, Mickey Catonni, and here are the twins, Davey and Derek Donato."

"Hi Mickey, Davey and Derek. Nice to meet you all."

"Thank you. Nice meeting you too, Mr. Rizzo," the boys all chimed in.

Laura and Dan stepped forward and exchanged introductions and were welcomed in by the Rizzo's and invited to sit in the living room for a drink and some hors d'oeuvres.

"You have a beautiful house, Jane! It's so stately and colorful. Quite impressive too." Laura announced as she sat down.

"Oh, thank you, Laura. It demands some work but now that Bob is home we can get some of it done." Jane looked over at her husband.

Bob smiled and rolled his eyes at his wife.

The kids were already helping themselves to some chips and dips and crackers and cheese. Mrs. Rizzo brought out shrimp cocktail and some mixed drinks of choice for the adults and soda for the kids.

The kids moved off after picking a little and went into the den aka library. The girls brought out the books that the ghost had given them and opened to the pages that they had read to share with the boys.

Abby and Holly filled Mickey in when he asked questions about their being more than one ghost.

"How do you know there are more than one ghost here?"

"Well, from the books it tells us that one ghost is from before the Sheridan's lived here. We are surmising that there are possibly two more ghosts, a little girl, Elena, who fell down the stairs and Mrs. Sheridan who also fell down the stairs."

"Oh, I see. Who did I feel when I was here the first time? It was a cold spot. I didn't actually see a ghost, but the eyes of the pictures appeared to be watching me. It was too creepy. I don't think I will look at them again," Mickey bristled and shook his arms as goosebumps were now visible there.

Davey spoke up to explain, "We think the cold spot was Mrs. Sheridan since she was too old to really display any strength like the others. The first ghost, Felicity, who Abby and Holly saw was the strongest in will because she actually carried over the two books and dropped them on their beds. The next ghost, the little girl, Elena, was only five years old and she appears to be the mischievous one who moves things around and hides them."

"Oh, I see. The younger you die the stronger you are as a ghost."

"Yes, I think you got it. Though Elena is too young to know that she is even dead. We think she wants to have all the things that Abby and Holly have. That's why she takes them. She could be hiding them somewhere in the passageways. Do you want to go check them before dinner?"

"Okay, let's go. I have the flashlight right here. Ready?" Abby handed it to Davey to lead the way.

The others followed close behind in line as Davey and Derek quietly opened the secret door in the wall behind the book shelves.

"Holly, does either Mrs. or Mr. Rizzo know about these passageways?"

"Shh, no, they don't. Abby doesn't want to tell them yet. She wants to find the stash that the ghost hid before telling her parents about it."

"Ha, does she think she will find buried treasure here?" Derek guffawed.

"No, I don't think so. But who knows what we will find, right?"

"Yeah, I guess anything is possible," Derek considered.

"Hey you two, be quiet," Mickey said. "You might scare the ghosts. Ha ha."

"Funny Mickey!" Derek laughed along with him.

The kids quieted down as they moved forward through the first door on the left and beyond Abby's secret door to the next door that led to Holly's room.

They passed through this door and looked along the wall for any opening or place where a mischievous ghost could hide her stash.

"Girls, look along the right side of the wall and we boys will look along the left side. If you find something let us know," Davey said in a whisper.

Abby whispered, "Okay. Don't go too far without us though. It's kind of creepy and dark here." Holly joined Abby feeling along the wall for any cracks or crevices where something could be hidden.

Abby jumped up in alarm as her fingers touched something in a little nook on the wall. "Look boys what I found? Here are my socks and scarf!"

Holly bent down to look closer as Davey shined the flashlight over the area. "Yep, looks like you found Elena's stash of stuff. What else is in there?" Everyone leaned in for a better look.

"Wow, looks like it's my book and pen," Holly announced in excitement.

"Wait a minute. There is something else in here," Derek reached in further and pulled out another book. It looked like another diary.

Derek took the flashlight from Davey and held it over the book. It appeared to be old and faded but the name was still legible – Endora.

"Who is Endora?" Mickey asked.

"She is one of the two girls who lived here before the Sheridan's. Her younger sister, Elena, is the one who fell down the cellar stairs," Abby explained.

"Let's go back and read it. Maybe it will tell us something else of importance," Holly added.

"Okay, but first I want to go further to find the door to your room, Holly. Don't you want to find it?" Abby walked ahead to search.

"Not really, Abby. Can't we go back? Your parents will be looking for us."

Holly looked around but Abby was nowhere in sight. "Abby, where are you? Boys, where's Abby?"

"Abby, come on, don't tease us," Davey called out clearly worried.

Mickey and Derek called her name too but she didn't answer.

They all walked forward extending the light back and forth along the walls until they came to an opening. They pushed on it and came into Holly's room.

"We found it! We found your room, Holly," the boys announced.

The boys looked around the room and behind them. Where was Holly?"

"Oh, boy, we're in trouble," Mickey stated in a stutter.

"Holly, Abby, where are you?" Davey, Derek and Cat called out.

"Stop kidding around, girls! Where are you?"

The boys went back into the passageway and flashed the light back and forth as they called out the girls' names.

They started going upward in the passageway away from Holly's room and came to another door. They opened the door and passed through to another corridor. This one suddenly dropped off and led down to a set of stairs. The boys called out for the girls once again.

As the boys were ready to turn around and go back they heard something at the bottom of the stairs.

"Did you hear that, Davey? Something is down there."

"Yes, I heard it. Let's go downstairs and find out what it is."

"Cat, are you coming too?"

"Um, I can wait here in case the girls come back."

"Okay, Cat, that sounds like a good idea," Derek agreed knowing the real reason Cat didn't want to go with them.

Davey called out again, "Abby, Holly, are you down there?"

CHAPTER SEVENTEEN

Surprising Discovery

From the kitchen, Jane Rizzo was calling the kids to dinner. She went into the den to look for them and noticed the shelf was pulled away from the wall. She peeked in and urgently called her husband.

"Robert, come quickly. There's a doorway in the wall behind the shelves in the den. The kids may have gone in there. You must find them. They could be hurt!"

"Okay, Jane. Don't worry. Can you get me the large flashlight? Dan and I will find them." Turning toward Dan, Robert motioned for him to follow.

"What's up Robert? Where are the kids?"

"I don't know Dan. Oh, please call me Bob. Jane always calls me Robert when she's nervous."

"Ah yeah, I know what that's like. I am Daniel when Laura is upset with me. Let's go find the kids."

Jane rushed out to the kitchen and rummaged around for the large flashlight. All she could find were the two smaller ones.

"I couldn't find the large flashlight but here are two smaller ones."

"Thanks Jane. Please relax. The kids couldn't have gotten far. They could be exploring, that's all."

Laura and Jane paced back and forth in the den waiting for their husbands to come back from the secret passageway.

"I can't believe that the girls didn't tell me about this secret doorway and the passageways! I'm shocked that they would even want to go exploring in there," Jane spoke clearly upset.

Laura responded in a calm voice, "I trust my boys to use good judgment. Don't worry. They will watch over the girls." Laura avoiding telling Jane that she knew about the passageways from her boys.

"Do you think the kids found the ghosts inside the doorway? Maybe that's why they went in," Jane responded anxiously.

"They could have seen something to make them go in. I'm sure it's awfully dark and gloomy in there," Laura agreed as she tried to keep her own nerves at bay.

In the passageway, Bob and Dan walked to the right calling out to the kids. They each held a flashlight and moved them out to the right and left. They noticed the corridor rising as they continued to walk upwards. There were two doors ahead. They opened the first and entered another corridor. They felt along the wall when they noticed a light under the base of the wall. They pushed and pushed against the wall until it gave and found themselves inside the kitchen.

They looked at each other in surprise. We should go back in there. There has to be another way to go."

"Yeah, you're right, Bob. Let's try going in the opposite direction. Maybe that's where the kids went."

The men quickly went back into the passageway and reversed their direction to follow the left passageway.

They didn't speak, intent on finding the kids before their wives came looking for them.

**

The twins used "TT" not only to calm themselves down but also to commune with Aunt Gigi and Mianna. It was evident that they required her help.

Derek, clear your mind and think about Aunt Gigi. We need her help.

Okay, already doing that, Bro.

Davey, Derek, I can hear and see you. What is the problem, boys? Did you lose something?

Yes, Aunt Gigi. We can't find the girls. We are going down to the cellar. Inside the wall we found a passageway, Davey reported.

Okay, I can see the stairs. Be careful. Put your flashlight in front of you. There, I see them.

Where? Where are they, Aunt Gigi? Derek asked.

Oh, my God, they're on the floor. They could have fallen. Please help us, Aunt Gigi!

Okay, be calm. I will be right here. Go over to them. They appear to be okay. I think they could have fainted. They're not hurt.

Thank you, Aunt Gigi. I'll try to wake them up.

Davey leaned down and lightly touched Abby's shoulder as Derek did the same to Holly.

Both girls came around and looked startled.

"What happened, girls? Are you okay?" Davey asked as he helped Abby up.

"I don't know, Davey. I followed the corridor and heard something when I got to the stairs. I thought it was Holly but she didn't answer."

"Abby, I followed the same way and heard something too. I thought it was you. The next minute I was at the bottom of the stairs and I don't remember anything else."

"Yes, I did the same thing, Holly. There was definitely something down here. It wanted us to come here. Maybe there is something down here the ghost wanted us to see."

"Are you okay, Holly?" Derek pulled Holly up from the dirt floor and helped brush off her clothes.

"I'm okay, Derek. That's all right. I'll clean myself off." Holly smiled and nodded her thanks.

Derek backed away feeling awkward that he couldn't do more for Holly.

The twins looked around the large basement for any clues as to what the ghost wanted the girls to see. There were old boxes piled high in the far corner and an old wardrobe that appeared to be locked.

The girls looked closely at a large trunk that was sitting next to the wardrobe. They beckoned the boys over.

"Hey boys, look at this! Do you think you can open it?"

Davey bent down and flashed the light over the top. There was a lock on it but it didn't look like it was closed. He pulled it apart with some help from Derek and they opened the rusty lid and looked inside.

"Wow, look at all these old clothes, Holly! We could have a fun time dressing up like the people who used to be here. The clothes are definitely ancient, maybe a hundred years old or so."

"Yeah, let's bring it upstairs. Can you boys help us carry it up the stairs? Hey, where's Mickey?"

The twins had forgotten all about him. He was still up at the top of the stairs. They called out to him, "Hey Mickey, come on down. We need some help to carry something."

"What? Did you call me, Derek?"

"Yeah, get down here pronto. We need your help. We found something."

Mickey came down the stairs as fast as he could while looking behind him one last time.

"What's wrong, Mickey? Did you see a ghost or something?" Derek guffawed.

"No, but I heard someone calling our names up there. It sounded like your dad and Abby's dad."

"Oh-oh, they found the doorway. We didn't close it, that's why."

The three boys lifted the trunk while the girls led the way back to the stairs. As they began to climb with the girls in the lead lighting the way they heard their father's anxious voice calling them.

"Dad, we're here. We are coming upstairs. Be there in a few," Davey called out.

"Davey, are you all okay?" Dan asked as he looked down the stairs at the boys coming up with a large object.

"Let us help you with that. What is it?" Bob enquired looking the object over.

"Thanks Dad," Davey and Derek chirped together.

"Abby, Holly, are you all right?" Her father questioned with relief in his eyes.

"Yes, Dad, we're fine," Abby said as she gave her dad a hug along with Holly.

"Come on, kids. Your mothers are wrecks. We should get you back before they both have heart attacks. Besides dinner is ready and will get cold."

Mickey's eyes got wider. "Did you say dinner is ready? Let's get going everybody. We don't want it to get cold."

Mickey ran up ahead and came out into the den where the ladies were nervously wringing their hands.

"Mickey, is everyone okay?" Jane asked in an unsteady voice.

"Oh yes, we are all great. Is dinner ready? I'll go clean up." Mickey raced off to the bathroom to freshen up.

As the dads and the twins and girls came out into the den they were hugged and squeezed in relief by their mothers.

"Oh my God, you kids scared us half to death. Are you sure you're okay?" Jane voiced her anxiety.

"Yes, we are all fine, Mom," Abby announced with a smile hiding her own nerves about what had transpired.

The dads moved the trunk into the den and put it in front of the couch.

"What is that, Robert?"

"The kids found it in the basement. We can look it over later. It's time to get cleaned up and eat. We don't want your dinner to spoil."

Everyone took turns getting cleaned up and went out to the kitchen where Jane and Laura had reheated the food and set it out. Mickey was already sitting down with his fork and knife in his hands.

"Well, look at you, Mickey. Are you that hungry?" Jane laughed clearly amused by his delighted face.

"I'm always hungry, Mrs. Rizzo," Mickey laughed waiting for the first course to begin.

Dinner was a success and everyone pushed away their plates as Jane brought out coffee and dessert.

Mickey was ready for the dessert and skipped the coffee preferring to have milk along with the rest of the kids.

Jane sipped her coffee and picked at her blueberry crumble. She watched the kids as they were enjoying their desserts and waited for a chance to ask a question or two.

"Holly, can you please tell me why you did not reveal this secret door in the den? How long have you known about it?"

Holly swallowed a mouthful and drank some milk before answering her mother.

"Sorry, Mom. I was planning to tell you about all of the doors and passageways. I wanted to find what the ghost was hiding in there first. We may have found something big with the trunk. Can we go look at it?"

"Finish up and bring your dish over to the dishwasher, dear. All of you can go. I'll clean up the rest. I am relieved that you are all okay. Please don't go in there again, okay?"

"Um, okay, Mom," Abby assented reluctantly.

The kids jumped up all anxious to check out the mysterious trunk. They also wanted to sit and read some of the diary which had taken a backseat.

The girls looked over the lacy clothes in the trunk as the boys sat and read the diary. Hats and parasols were pulled out along with bloomers and wide hoops to go under fancy gowns.

The boys' heads were more into the diary and less into what the girls were modeling for them.

Davey and Derek read through a few pages and stopped and looked at each other sharing "TT" before telling the others what they had read.

CHAPTER EIGHTEEN

More Discoveries

Look, Davey. We have to tell the girls this. I can't believe it!

Okay, let's share. They'll want to know this too.

"Listen to this, girls and Mickey. This diary is Endora's but it is many years after the other one. You won't believe this!" Davey announced.

The girls dropped their hats and stepped out of their gowns as they sat down next to the twins waiting for more.

"What is it Davey?" Abby probed.

Holly sat down and Mickey came to sit on the other side of the twins. They all waited with baited breath for some new revelation.

"Okay, as we already know, Endora was the older sister of Elena who died in this house after falling down the stairs. But what you don't know is…"

"Davey, cut it out," Mickey cried in exasperation.

"Okay, sorry. Do you remember Mrs. Sheridan?"

"Yes, yes, we do, Davey," Abby and Holly responded agitated as Mickey by this time.

Derek stepped in to calm everyone down. "What Davey is trying to say is…there is a connection between Elena and Mrs. Sheridan."

"What connection? Oh, I know, Derek. They both fell down the cellar stairs," Abby announced.

"Well, that's true. But those two accidents happened quite a few years apart."

"Okay, we know that. What is the connection?" the girls yelled out together.

"Okay, okay, I'm getting there. According to this diary the Enders family left this house and moved away. Endora talks about how her family couldn't face the idea of being in this house any longer. But Endora and her brother Ethan felt responsible for their sister's accident. Endora detailed what had happened.

We were playing hide and seek and I was 'it.'
I counted and listened for footsteps to
determine where Ethan and Elena were

going to hide. I heard Ethan direct Elena to the cellar. She started to cry because she was afraid of the cellar. She said there was a ghost down there, a lady. Ethan called her a baby and said he was going to hide down there. If she didn't go with him he would tell me what a baby she really was. I know Elena looked up to me. I stopped counting when I heard a scream. I ran as fast as I could to the cellar and heard Ethan call out to Elena. I pushed him aside on the stairs as I brought a lighted candle with me. There at the bottom of the stairs was my sister. She wasn't moving. I bent down and touched her and shook her shoulder but she didn't move. I yelled at Ethan to get Mother and Father quickly. He ran back upstairs and I could hear him yelling out to Mother and Father. They all came back and Father picked up Elena and brought her back upstairs as Mother called the doctor. Ethan was crying and so was I. We feared that our dear little sister was dead.

"Oh my God, that is terrible," Abby cried with tears running down her face and Holly joined in.

"Wait, that is not all. There is more later on," Davey reported.

Everyone waited for Davey to continue as they held their breaths.

Endora continued many years later.

We moved away from where Elena had died. I could not forgive myself. I felt as if her death was my fault. Ethan couldn't deal with it either. He moved away after finishing school and married and had a family. I eventually married too but never could have children. I think God punished me for not taking better care of my sister. I felt compelled to come back here. I bought the house that was still available after we moved out. No one wanted to live here because of the ghost. I knew who the ghost was, my sister. I wanted to put her to rest. I would do what I could. I would go to the place where she took her last breath.

I have been living here for more than fifty years. I can feel her presence here but I still haven't seen the ghost of my sister. Maybe I am mistaken.

My husband is a kind and gentle man and has had much patience with me through all this. He gives me all his attention and love and watches over me. He is getting on in age too.

I am getting feebler and can't go up and down the stairs as well as I used to. But I will try one more time to reach Elena. I must tell her I'm sorry and release her to the other side. I hope to see her there one day soon. Endora Sheridan

"Davey, what else does it say?" Abby asked still wiping her tears.

Davey looked up from the page and stared at the group as he tried to get his breath.

"You won't believe this but Endora is or was Mrs. Sheridan. Mrs. Sheridan was Elena's sister!"

"Oh my God! No wonder they are still here together," Derek said feeling shocked.

"This is the last entry. There is no more. Endora, most likely, went down the cellar stairs and fell. Maybe she did finally see her sister but couldn't get her to go to the other side. She joined her here for eternity instead. It could have been a way to punish herself further," Davey surmised.

"Wow that is a surprise!" Abby said as she looked at everyone's shocked faces.

Cat spoke up after minutes of dead silence by all, "Wait a minute, Davey. How are you going to capture the ghosts?"

Derek nodded to Davey and answered Cat's question, "We need to talk to the ghosts. Maybe we can implore Endora to bring her sister along."

"What about the other ghost. Wait, when you read her diary Endora did mention another ghost down the cellar. Elena was frightened of a ghost in the cellar," Holly added.

"Yes, I remember that too, Davey," Abby said excitedly. "Maybe that's why the little girl fell. She lost her balance when she saw the woman ghost."

"Ah, yes that could explain the reason she fell," Cat responded.

"We should go back into the passageway where we found Elena's stash and call out to her and Endora to come to us. I will have the ghost flasher ready."

"Ghost flasher? What's a ghost flasher?" Abby and Holly asked jointly in confusion.

"Oh, sorry. We didn't tell you about this. Our Aunt Gigi let us borrow it to capture the ghosts."

The girls came over for a closer look as Davey pulled it out of his back pocket.

"Wow that is cool, Davey. You have a super cool aunt to have things like this. Is she a ghost hunter?" Abby touched it carefully.

"Yes, she is cool but not a ghost hunter. She said someone in her family in the past used it to exorcise a ghost. It hasn't been done for years. I hope this works. But Aunt Gigi assured us that it would," Davey nodded and smiled at Derek.

"Okay are we ready everyone?"

"Yes!" everyone answered more than ready to get this over with.

The group headed back into the passageway toward the first door on the right and beyond until they found the area where the nook was located. They stood side by side in a line and waited for Davey to begin.

Davey and Derek cleared their minds and opened them to Aunt Gigi and Mianna.

Aunt Gigi, we are inside the passageway where the stash of Elena was found. This may be the last place she visited. What should we do to bring her here? Davey asked.

Tell her about Mrs. Sheridan being Elena's sister.

What did you say, Derek? Mrs. Sheridan is Endora? Yes, I think I do remember her name being Endora. Sorry, I didn't make the connection. Thought it was merely a coincidence with the name.

Call out to Endora first, then Elena. Once you get one to come forward the other will follow and so will Felicity and the other ghosts from the pictures.

The group was watching Davey and Derek as they used "TT" not knowing what was going on until Mickey spoke up, "Oh, don't worry, the twins are working it all out in their heads. They use twin speak or twin telepathy."

"What? They can talk inside each other's heads? Wow, that is so cool! I wish we could do that, Holly. But I guess you are required be twins to do that. We're only cousins, so we're out of luck."

"Yeah, I guess so, Abby."

"Shh, you guys. We're working here," Derek warned with a smile.

"Sorry, Derek," Holly responded with a sweet smile of her own.

Davey began to call out, "Elena, Endora, please show yourselves. We know who you are and want to help you. We can release you from your prison here and send you over to the other side. Please come out."

The kids waited holding their breaths as they looked around and up and down the passageways around them. They were almost ready to give up when they began to feel a coldness emanating around them.

Cat spoke up in a shaky voice, "Uh-oh, I think Endora is here!"

"Endora, is that you? Please convince Elena to come forward too. We want to help you both. You have been here long enough. It is time for you to go to the other side and be together for eternity with the rest of your family. They are all waiting for you," Davey explained.

The coldness increased frightening the kids as they gathered closer together to stay warm. Shivering with chattering teeth and goosebumps the kids waited not sure this was a good idea after all.

Davey yelled out louder, "Elena, come out and show yourself. Endora is waiting for you. She wants you to go to the other side with her to join the family. You should come out now."

A willowy wisp of what looked like smoke appeared and circled around the group. It spun up and around their heads in a whimsical way until it slowed down and appeared in front of them.

The girls jumped back in alarm when they saw the ghost's face smiling at them. The coldness around them became warmed suddenly and appeared to embrace the little ghost until they were one.

Davey pulled out the ghost flasher and aimed it at the two ghosts which were entwined as one. Along came another entity with long flowing hair to join them and behind her were several more wisps of smoke.

"Oh, it's Felicity, David. She's here! Look, there are more ghosts behind her!" Abby exclaimed as she nodded at the spirit and backed away.

Davey smiled and pointed the ghost flasher toward the many specters, pressed the red button and silently prayed that it would work. He looked at the tube which was turning blue and pressed down the yellow button to contain the entities.

Davey and Derek sighed in relief as the group looked on in awe.

"Did you get them all, Davey?" Abby whispered.

"Yes, I think I did. They are now contained. We should get them outside the house immediately so they can go to the other side."

But before Davey could move he felt the flasher getting hotter and heavier to the touch. He looked at Derek and pleaded silently for help.

What's wrong, Davey?

I don't know!

It suddenly got hotter and heavier. I need your help to hold it before I lose it altogether.

Okay, no problem.

Derek gripped the flasher next to Davey's hands and they both walked out to the front door.

Cat watched the boys as they appeared to be laboring to hold onto the device.

"Do you guys want my help?"

"No, I think we got this now, Mickey. Thanks though," Davey nodded and smiled through clenched teeth.

"Yay, let's go outside quickly," Abby still whispered afraid to upset the whole operation.

The group walked outside and watched as Derek helped Davey press the buttons in order. They all stood back as the tube turned clear again and the ghosts floated up into the air and turned to look at the group. The kids could see three faces wide with smiles and trails of smoke behind them as they floated up, up and away.

"Phew! I can't believe that happened, guys!" Mickey declared still feeling like he was dreaming the whole thing.

"Wow that was awesome, Davey and Derek!" Abby said in an excited voice.

"Yeah, that was incredible that you did that!" Holly exclaimed too thrilled to say anything more.

"Boy am I glad that it worked!" Davey said with relief in his voice.

"Yeah, me too, Bro."

Looking out the window at the group were the adults. Jane opened the door and called out, "Hey kids, what are you doing outside?"

"Did you see what happened, Mom?"

"I saw you all looking up. What did you see?"

"Davey and Derek released the ghosts, Mom. Would you believe it?"

"Really, that was what you were all looking at? What did they look like?"

"They were white and wispy like clouds with faces. They even smiled at us. I think they were happy to be released."

"Well, that is amazing. I wish I could have seen them too."

Laura, Dan and Bob joined in and began asking questions about how the boys performed this magic.

Davey and Derek explained and smiled, proud of their accomplishment.

Hey Davey, we forgot to let Aunt Gigi know what we did.

Not to worry boys, I saw what you did! You were magnificent! Very proud of you!

Congratulations on your first official ghost flasher success!

Thanks, Aunt Gigi, the boys retorted.

Everyone went back in and sat around with the adults to discuss the ghosts and their findings about Elena and Mrs. Sheridan. The twins left out the parts that involved magic words and incantations from Aunt Gigi. They didn't want the Rizzo's to know that their aunt was a witch or that they were warlocks. That fact would frighten the Rizzo's who would bar them from Abby and Holly forever.

Overall it was a successful night for the kids. The adults enjoyed themselves and got to know each other better. They promised to get together again soon.

After many thanks were shared, the Donato's and Mickey dispersed to their car.

The twins shared their excitement once they dropped Cat off at his house.

Wow, what a night, Davey!

It was so much fun, wasn't it, Derek!

I can't believe we did!

Yeah, even Aunt Gigi was excited for us.

I'm tired, how about you, Derek?

Yeah, let's write our findings on the board and call it a night.

Right, I'm so ready.

Let's call Abby tomorrow, Derek, to see how the girls are doing without ghosts.

Smiles all around as their father drove into the garage and everyone jumped out.

Tomorrow would be the test. The twins would call Abby and find out if the ghosts were really gone.

CHAPTER NINETEEN

Case Closed

Sunday dawned early for Derek but not for Davey. Derek was up and raring to go. Derek made as much noise in his room as possible to wake up his brother.

"For God's sake, Derek! What in the world are you doing? I'm trying to sleep here!"

"Oh, sorry, Bro. I was looking for something in my closet and bureau," he announced as he once again slammed the drawers with gusto wearing his usual smirk.

"Take off that smirk, Derek! I can see it from here!"

"You can? No, you're kidding, right?"

Davey laughed, "Ha, that will keep you wondering if I can see it or not."

Slowly moving out of bed, Davey swung his legs off the bed and stood up stretching like a cat. He searched through his closet for his Sunday clothes to attend church. It was still early but at least his mother wouldn't have to call him to hurry up. He would surprise her and be ready an hour ahead.

Derek strolled into his brother's room to see if he really was up. If not, he had plans to coax Davey a little more.

"Oh, you are up, Davey."

"Hmm, yes, I am. Mom will be calling soon for us to go down for breakfast. I plan to surprise her and go down before she does call."

"Wow, she may think that you are sick or something."

"Hey Derek, listen. We need to call Abby when we get back from church to see how she is doing. According to Aunt Gigi the flasher always works if used properly."

The boys fidgeted, keeping under their mother's watchful eye, all during church anxious to get back home to call Abby.

The minute their father shut the engine of the car in the garage the boys jumped out but were stopped in their tracks by their mother.

"Where are you two going in such a hurry? I noticed you were restless in church. I expect better behavior from you at your age. Don't do that again. Do you hear me?" Laura's face was showing her sternest expression of displeasure.

"Sorry, Mom. We were thinking about Abby and Holly and were worried about how they were doing. We didn't mean to be so restless," Davey apologized.

"Yeah, Mom, sorry about that. It won't happen again."

"You bet it won't happen again!" Laura gave the boys 'the look' that they feared.

"Yes Mom," the boys responded in unison.

Oh boy, we're in trouble, Davey!

You're telling me!

Do you think Mom will let us call Abby?

Do you want to ask her, Davey?

Umm, I think I'll give her a few minutes.

Let's go upstairs and change into our jeans so we can take Aggy out for a run.

Aggy heard her name and came running up the stairs and into Davey's room.

"Hi Ag, how are you doing, girl? Give me a minute. Let me change."

Derek finished changing first, grabbed Aggy, and headed back downstairs. He called out to Davey, "You call Abby, Bro. I'll be outside with Aggy."

Davey groaned as he went out to the kitchen where his mother was emptying out the dishwasher.

"Um, Mom, sorry to bother you. But, um, can I call Abby?"

Laura turned and faced Davey but 'the look' was no longer there. She sighed and said, "Okay, Davey. But I'll want your help afterwards."

"Sure, whatever you want, Mom," Davey sighed in relief. He would do anything to not see that look again.

Abby picked up the phone and sounded perky. "Hi Davey. How are you? Thanks so much for helping us yesterday."

"Oh, you're welcome, Abby. That's why I was calling. I wanted to know if there were any problems. Did the ghosts come back?"

"No, things were very quiet. Holly even went back to her own room."

"It was so cool what you did, Davey. I wish we had more ghosts so I could watch you do it again!"

"Um, well, I think once was enough, but thank you, Abby." Davey blushed relieved that Abby couldn't see his face.

"Well, I'll see you on Monday, Davey. Look forward to it. Lunch at the same table?" Abby asked eagerly.

"Oh sure. See you on Monday, same table." Davey smile grew wider.

"Bye, Davey."

"Yeah, bye, Abby."

Davey put the phone back on the wall and his smile was still plastered on his face as he went outside to see Derek and Aggy playing in the yard.

"Hey Davey. Did you call Abby?"

"Yep, all's clear. It looks like another case is successfully closed, Derek."

Feel's good, doesn't it, Bro?"

"Sure does, Derek."

"We should call Aunt Gigi and report everything went as planned, shouldn't we, Davey?"

As Davey was going to answer, the boys both heard in their heads, *It's not necessary to call me, boys. The line is still open in your minds. I can hear you. Great job! Congratulations again, boys! Another job well done – see you tomorrow after school.*

Okay, Aunt Gigi. Thanks, the boys answered together.

The twins closed off their minds and spoke out loud.

"That was disturbing, huh, Bro?"

"Sure was, Derek!"

"We should close off our minds or Aunt Gigi will be inside them all the time, ugh," Davey said feeling creeped out.

"I agree, Davey!"

"That is too weird to even think about!"

The twins laughed until tears came into their eyes. They slapped high fives and went to chase Aggy around the yard once again.

The boys knew they would require Aunt Gigi's help on more cases but for now, they were on their own and having fun.

THE END

A NOTE FROM THE AUTHOR

Thank you for purchasing one of Jemsbooks. A review would be greatly appreciated wherever you purchased it. Please go to my website for more children's books: http://www.jemsbooks.com.

As with all Jemsbooks the stories are purely a product of my imagination and cannot be copied in any way or used for any purpose.

This is the fifth book in this middle-grade series. I plan to write a few more of these books in the next year or two.

My themes deal in life lessons and teaching children how to be polite, kind and sensitive to others' feelings. I want children to know that it is okay to be different. It is extremely important that all children feel safe and loved in their homes and in their lives.

These stories are mainly to entertain, delight and teach children about life lessons and for the sheer joy of reading. I hope your children will enjoy these magical stories and learn valuable lessons that will stay with them for a lifetime.

Look for a new series for girls, Abby and Holly, coming in 2018 and a YA fantasy series coming in 2018 and 2019.

Reading Gives You Wings to Fly! Soar with Jemsbooks!

With Blessings & Love,
Janice Spina

ABOUT THE AUTHOR

Janice Spina is a retired administrative secretary from a school system in Massachusetts. She has always loved writing poetry and children's stories.

This is the fifth book in this middle-grade series. Janice has published nine children's books for Preschool-Grade 3. She has published two novels and a short story collection under J.E. Spina. She continues to write more children's books and is in the process of editing more books for publication.

Janice has received three Pinnacle Book Achievements Awards and a Reader's Favorite Award for this series. Her children's book, ***Lamby the Lonely Lamb***, has received a Mom's Choice Award, and ***Jerry the Crabby Crayfish***, has received a Pinnacle Book Achievement Award.

Her next projects are a YA series for girls which will be a spin-off from this book and writing a sequel to her first novel, *Hunting Mariah*.

Look for more Jemsbooks on her website

http://www.jemsbooks.com

Amazon Author Page for all Jemsbooks:
http://amazon.com/author/janicespina7

Follow her on:

Twitter: http://twitter.com/janice_spina

Facebook Main Page:
http://www.facebook.com/janice.spina.9

FB Author Page:
http//www.facebook.com/janicespina7

FB Novelist Page:
http://www.facebook.com/jespina77

LinkedIn:
http://www.linkedin.com/pub/janice-spina/59/321/a01/

She also has a blog
http://www.jemsbooks.wordpress.com

She reviews books and talks about her venture in writing and publishing, travels, and authors' guest posts and interviews.

Janice lives in New Hampshire with her husband, John, who is her illustrator and cover creator.

Janice's slogan is: ***Reading Gives You Wings to Fly!***

ABOUT THE ILLUSTRATOR

Dr. John Spina is a retired elementary and middle school principal from a school system in Massachusetts with a doctorate in education.

John has illustrated and created covers for nine children's books for PS-Grade 3. This is the fifth book in this middle-grade series he has illustrated. He also created the covers for Janice's two novels, *Hunting Mariah* and *How Far Is Heaven* and short story collection, *An Angel Among Us*, all of which she wrote under J.E. Spina.

John is currently working on illustrating more of Janice's books and covers. He is Janice's most avid supporter and without his assistance she couldn't continue to do all that she has done.

Their joint goal is to encourage children of all ages to read.